"Anyone home?" called a deep voice.

Looking across the kitchen, Aveline was astonished to see Lucas in the doorway. His bare forearms were scratched, and mosquito bites dotted his skin. Mud clung to his boots and trousers, and his suspenders were twisted over his torn shirt.

"What happened to you?" she asked. "Why haven't you changed out of the dirty clothes you wore yesterday?"

"These are different dirty clothes," he replied. Motioning toward the back porch, he added, "I can show you faster than I can tell you."

Aveline frowned, troubled by how his eyes glittered with merriment. She'd seen that when he was about to launch a battery of flirting. If she had the nerve, she'd tell him to be on his way, that she didn't have any time or interest in playing his games. If *Mamm* caught wind of how Lucas had paid attention to her, matchmaking would go into highest gear.

Yet she couldn't restrain her curiosity…

Jo Ann Brown loves stories with happily-ever-after endings. A former military officer, she is thrilled to write about finding that forever love all over again with her characters. She and her husband (her real hero who knows how to fix computer problems quickly when she's on deadline) divide their time between Western Massachusetts and Amish country in Pennsylvania. She loves hearing from readers, so drop her a note at joannbrownbooks.com.

Books by Jo Ann Brown

Love Inspired

Amish of Prince Edward Island

Building Her Amish Dream
Snowbound Amish Christmas
Caring for Her Amish Neighbor
Unexpected Amish Protectors

Green Mountain Blessings

An Amish Christmas Promise
An Amish Easter Wish
An Amish Mother's Secret Past
An Amish Holiday Family

Amish Spinster Club

The Amish Suitor
The Amish Christmas Cowboy
The Amish Bachelor's Baby
The Amish Widower's Twins

Visit the Author Profile page at LoveInspired.com for more titles.

Unexpected
Amish Protectors

Jo Ann Brown

LOVE INSPIRED
INSPIRATIONAL ROMANCE

LOVE INSPIRED®

INSPIRATIONAL ROMANCE

Recycling programs
for this product may
not exist in your area.

ISBN-13: 978-1-335-59864-6

Unexpected Amish Protectors

Copyright © 2024 by Jo Ann Ferguson

For questions and comments about the quality of this book, please contact us
at CustomerService@Harlequin.com.

Love Inspired
22 Adelaide St. West, 41st Floor
Toronto, Ontario M5H 4E3, Canada
www.LoveInspired.com

Printed in U.S.A.

Let not mercy and truth forsake thee:
bind them about thy neck;
write them upon the table of thine heart:
So shalt thou find favour and
good understanding in the sight of God and man.
Trust in the Lord with all thine heart;
and lean not unto thine own understanding.
—*Proverbs* 3:3–5

For Don Horning
the first to welcome us to Amish country

Chapter One

❦

Prince Edward Island, Canada

Lucas Kuepfer was in a bad mood as he drove
along the road paralleling the Brudenell River,
heading home after picking up supplies in Montague on the other side of the headland. Being
in a bad mood wasn't unusual for him as summer came to an end. He couldn't remember the
last time he'd been in a *gut* mood. He should be
happy. His brother, who'd been blinded in an accident earlier in the year, was regaining his sight.
Lucas's crops were almost ready to harvest. His
cousin's farm was productive as was the family's farm shop.

Everything should have been great.

Everything had been more awful than usual
since, while having breakfast that morning, he'd
read *The Diary*, the monthly magazine for Old

Order communities. It'd brought back the pain that should have been put aside before he'd left Ontario. He'd done everything he could to leave his broken heart behind, but nothing had worked. Other people, including his brother, Juan, and his cousins who'd moved with him to Prince Edward Island two years ago, would have been shocked he was still nursing the pain of being tossed aside by the woman he'd hoped to marry the year before they left.

The problem was the woman, Robin Boshart, had wanted to marry someone else. Anyone else, as she'd told him the last time they'd spoken, because anybody else would have been more fun than Lucas. Apparently she'd found that someone because her wedding had been listed in the most recent edition of *The Diary*. Robin's *mamm* was the scribe for his former community, so details of the wedding and the large number of guests had filled the letter.

A motion among the trees to his right caught his eye. An animal or a person? He kept his gaze on the road that glistened from the rain they'd had earlier. Another sign of how depressed he was. Usually, Lucas would have been eager to figure out what was wandering close to the road. He kept a journal of the animals and birds he'd seen in Prince Edward Island.

Today, he didn't care.

"What does it matter?" He grimaced. He was turning into a grump, proving Robin right. If he—

Someone ran through a break in the hedge to his right. Someone heading straight into the path of his buggy. Someone not very tall. A woman. Or was it a *kind*?

Lucas yanked to the left on the reins, turning Rebel toward the center of the road. The driver of an oncoming truck hammered his horn. He was on a collision path with the buggy. Lucas pulled the reins in the other direction. The buggy's metal wheels slid. The truck's brakes squealed and the tires spun as the vehicle began to skid. Praying he wasn't going to get them killed, Lucas shouted to Rebel to head for the shoulder.

Where was the person who'd jumped out in front of him?

The buggy tilted. He held his breath as its wheels hit the soft dirt beyond the shoulder. Rebel danced as the buggy jerked to a stop, one corner striking the hedge.

Lucas jumped out. Running to his horse, he worked to calm him as the truck honked angrily again and zoomed by. His heart beat like storm-driven waves on the shore. Where was the pedestrian? He hadn't felt the buggy's wheels hit anything other than the edge of the road. Was the person okay?

He looked both ways but saw nobody. Tall

trees blocked the view of the river to his left, and a golf course was visible past the high hedges on his right. Had someone pushed their way from the course to look for an errant ball?

"Moonbeam!" he heard someone call. "Moonbeam, *komm* here. Tweet-tweet-tweet! Tweet-tweet-tweet!"

A woman, he realized, when he walked around Rebel and saw her on the road. She was barely five feet tall. The sunlight on her hair made it appear as bright red as the soil. Her conical *kapp* was askew and she straightened it as she put her hand to her brow to scan the trees across the road. They marked the edge of the marsh leading to a cove in the river.

"Are you all right?" she asked as he approached.

"*Ja.* You?"

She raised her head and he drew in a sharp breath. Aveline Lampel! He should have guessed. The Lampel women had a reputation for being pushy and having their noses in everyone else's business. He could imagine either Aveline or her *mamm* stepping out into traffic and assuming everyone would stop. A plain woman usually didn't think she was the center of the universe, but Aveline's *mamm*, Chalonna, seemed to believe she was. After hearing how Aveline had approached his cousin and cajoled him—or to hear Mark tell it, *cornered* him—into asking her to go with him to a benefit supper, Lucas had made sure to avoid her.

Until now.

"Have you lost your mind?" he demanded. "Didn't you see me and the truck?"

"I'm sorry. I've lost a calf, and I need to get her before she's injured."

"You won't find her if you get yourself killed. What's wrong with you?"

He heard her sharp intake of breath. His words had been harsh. *Ja*, she'd made a mistake, but he shouldn't be dumping his grim feelings on her. She wasn't Robin.

Aveline drew herself up to her full height, but the top of her head didn't reach his shoulder. "Nothing is wrong with me, Lucas Kuepfer. I'm trying to find a wayward calf. I don't need your interference."

"It sounds like you need my help if you're chasing a calf and sounding like a bird."

"A bird?"

"Tweet-tweet-tweet," he said as she had.

For a moment, a smile lit her face, transforming it. "I was saying 'treat-treat-treat.' It's a signal for her to know I've got something special to share with her." Then she grew serious. "Did you see a calf on the road?"

"What kind of calf?" He tried to remember which breed of cattle the Lampels raised to make the cheese they sold at farmers' markets. "Jersey? Brown Swiss?"

"Water buffalo."

He stared at her, shocked. A water buffalo? In Prince Edward Island? Was she trying to make him look like a fool?

"Excuse me?" he asked. "What did you say?"

Aveline Lampel should have been accustomed to how people looked at her as if she'd announced she was going to flap her arms and fly over the Island. Water buffalo were a rare breed in eastern Canada, but she'd convinced her *daed* to let her buy a small herd after the family had moved to Prince Edward Island four years ago. The first calf had been born at winter's end and two others later in spring. The milk was a great addition to the family's cheese-making business. Homemade mozzarella was rare in Canada, and they had a long list of customers waiting to buy the delicious cheese.

She didn't have time to explain to Lucas Kuepfer as they stood on the Georgetown road. He appeared eager to be anywhere but with her. She'd be as happy to put an end to this conversation because she had a job to do.

Lifting her eyes farther, because Lucas was a foot taller than she was, she ignored his dark *gut* looks that were, she'd been told, inherited from his *grossmammi* who'd been born in Mexico. Or she tried to pay them no attention. It wasn't easy not to let her gaze linger on his high cheekbones and brows arching above his dark brown eyes like a pair of black swans. His hair, swept from his forehead by the warm breeze, was as ebony.

"You're raising water buffalo?" he asked, his deep voice resonating along the road.

"*Ja.*" She checked her pocket to make sure she hadn't lost the alfalfa cubes. She needed them to lure the calf back to the herd. "I've got to go. I must find Moobeam."

As she took a step toward the far side of the road, Lucas asked, "Was that whom you were calling for? A water buffalo calf named Moonbeam?"

She paused. It wouldn't be polite to walk away when he'd asked her a direct question. Besides, as she and *Daed* had discussed many times, educating their neighbors about water buffalo was a *gut* thing. Others might decide to raise the animals and sell their *millich* to the Lampels for making cheese.

"Her name is Moobeam," Aveline replied.

"That's what I said. Moonbeam."

She shook her head, wondering if he was being obtuse on purpose. With his reputation for teasing and flirting with every woman he'd ever met, he might think he was being witty. She thought he was as thick as the asphalt under her feet.

"*Moo*beam," she corrected, emphasizing the first syllable. "You know, like the sound a cow makes. Moo."

"You named a cow *Moo*beam?"

"Why not?"

He stared at her as if he couldn't think of a reply.

She didn't have time for him to find one. Taking another step across the road, she said, "I need to catch her before she gets mired in the marsh or worse."

"Don't water buffalo like water?"

"They do, but a calf on its own can get hurt." Aveline had reached the far side of the road when Lucas called her name. "I've got to go, Lucas. If Moobeam gets stuck, she could struggle to escape and break a leg."

"Let me help you."

She wanted to say no, to tell him she was capable of finding a wandering calf on her own, but she didn't. She and her *daed* hoped the second generation of their small herd would be healthy and productive. Making sure the calf was safe was too important to let personalities get in the way.

"*Danki*. I'd appreciate that."

"Where did you see her last?"

"Heading into the trees." She pointed at the

ones in front of her. "*Komm mol*. She can move fast when she's inclined."

Aveline reached for a tree's slender trunk for balance as she slid partway into the deep ditch beyond the road's shoulder. She wanted to jump across and avoid the water swirling at the bottom. Maybe if she and Lucas helped each other, they could keep their shoes dry.

She was about to say that when she realized he'd returned to his buggy. Had he decided not to assist her? Was his offer only an attempt to charm her? She hadn't imagined he'd be insincere when a neighbor needed help.

Then he pulled something out and draped it over his left shoulder. As he crossed the road in a few long strides, she saw it was a length of rope.

"I don't think lassoing a water buffalo is a *gut* idea," she said. "Moobeam's horns are small, and throwing a rope will spook her."

He chuckled, a warm, generous sound. "I wasn't planning on playing cowboy. I'll leave that to my cousin Daryn who wants to herd cattle on the range. I figured if we can catch your Moobeam, putting her on a leash might help get her home."

She nodded, ashamed. He was being kind. Being real instead of making everything a flirting game. How many young women had she heard complaining about him? She should know better than to heed others' reputations. She wasn't like her own reputation. She wasn't desperate to be married. Not in the least. She was focused on building her herd and living a quiet life that wasn't interrupted by the callers her *mamm* despaired would never come to their door.

Mamm fretted about Aveline being without a boyfriend or a fiancé or, most important, a husband. It had gotten worse since Aveline's older brothers, Dwayne and Wes, had revealed they were planning to marry after the harvest. *Mamm* wasn't shy about asking embarrassing questions to family or friends. Even strangers were subjected to *Mamm*'s concerns that Aveline wasn't encouraging a man to propose.

Aveline had almost blurted out that might have happened if her family hadn't moved to Prince Edward Island. Merle Shenk had been starting to notice her as he hadn't when they'd been scholars together. His smile had changed from teasing to something warmer. Before anything could develop beyond a smile and a wink, *Daed* had whisked *Mamm*, Aveline and her two older brothers east.

She loved the Island with its red-soil vistas and the pulsing ocean waves. White clapboard houses and barns and Quonset huts and greenhouses marked the farms that seemed to have stepped out of a simpler time. What a wondrous place to launch a new and innovative type of farming! That was what she must focus on. Not the what-ifs of a relationship that had been over before it began. Yet she couldn't keep from thinking about what her life would have been like if they hadn't moved.

"Let me," Lucas said as he held out his right hand. "Hold on and jump. I won't let you fall."

"Okay." She held her breath, hoping she didn't slip on the slick grass and tumble into the ditch.

Lucas was as *gut* as his word. She gripped his work-roughened hand and leaped from one side of the ditch to the other. Her fingers tightened on his as she fought for balance on the wet grass.

"Got it?" he asked.

"*Ja*." She started to release his hand.

"Not yet. I don't want to land in the water either."

Wondering how he expected her to keep that from happening, she nodded.

"Plant your feet," he ordered.

"Okay," she repeated, rubbing her soaked black sneakers into the grass until the soles were against earth. "Go ahead."

She held her breath, but he moved with a grace she hadn't expected such a tall man to possess. His feet didn't slip as he landed right next to her, but his arms windmilled, almost knocking her over with the rope.

Throwing her arms around him, she closed her eyes, praying they wouldn't fall in the muddy water. He slid a couple centimeters, and she was drawn closer to the water with him; then he steadied her.

She released him. The last thing she needed was to have someone driving by and seeing her with her arms around the notorious flirt. *Mamm* would decide it was necessary to talk to the deacon about arranging a marriage ceremony.

"Let's get going," she said as she grasped the top of the ditch's wall and pulled herself up. Wiping her hands on her apron, she regarded it with a grimace. She was thankful she'd put on her oldest one before checking on the herd. The black polyester was filthy and one corner was torn. She must have caught it in the hedge.

It was his turn to say, "Okay." He shifted the rope on his shoulder and waved his hand in an indeterminate direction. "Lead the way."

She did, heading for the trees. They grew closer together, knit with knee-high underbrush that tried to keep her out. She held the branches until Lucas took them, not wanting them to snap back at him. Birdsong flooded the morning air and the shrill buzz of insects warned she might be covered by mosquito bites before she found the calf.

If she found the calf...

Aveline picked her way through the bushes. Where was Moobeam? None of the others in the herd could have fit through the hole the calf had found in the fence, but Aveline suspected the others wouldn't have pushed through to discover what was on the far side.

Lucas examined the ground and Aveline paused. She held her breath, listened to the singing birds and the soft breeze gliding through the leaves and the quick zip of insects.

Was that a rustle?

Not of tree leaves. Something closer to the ground.

She grasped Lucas's shoulder. When he looked at her, shocked at her bold motion, she put her finger to her lips. The fallen trees in front of them were bleached white by salt and time. Bushes had grown into a tangled cocoon around them.

"There," she whispered.

"Where?"

She pointed to the deadfall. "Over there. I heard something moving."

Uncoiling the rope from his shoulder, he motioned for her to take the lead. He must think Moobeam would be less likely to bolt if she saw someone she knew.

Aveline almost laughed. The calf wasn't that mature yet. She came running when Aveline appeared by the fence, because Moobeam knew she'd get a treat. Otherwise, the calf ignored her. Reaching into her apron pocket, she pulled out an alfalfa cube. It offered her the best chance to get close enough to grab the calf.

She edged forward. Twigs cracked under her feet. Something small scurried away, rattling the underbrush. A much larger form crashed through the greenery beyond the fallen trees. Knowing she couldn't wait longer, she ran around the windfall.

Arms were flung around her, knocking her off her feet. She landed hard on the ground and winced. What was going on? A calf didn't have arms.

"You're here!" cried a girl's voice from beside her. "Thank God, you're here at last!"

Aveline sat up and stared at the *kind* beside her. Though the girl's blonde hair was as snarled as the branches around them, her bright blue eyes were awash with the tears pouring down her face. Had the *kind* been hurt when she'd bowled them over? The youngster, who looked to be eleven or twelve years old, wore a filthy pink T-shirt with a large colorful fish on the front, a pair of torn jeans and once-white sneakers flecked with gold and black paint.

Aveline looked at Lucas, who had paused by the roots of the fallen trees. He was rolling the rope over his shoulder, his mouth in a grim line.

She understood why when she saw cold embers from a campfire. Discarded cans and wrappers had been tossed everywhere. Her nose wrinkled at an odor that lingered in the air, the stench of rotten food and unwashed bodies. When her gaze settled on the girl in front of her, she saw dirt caked on her hands and face. How long had the *kind* been out here on her own?

Or had she been alone? Cigarette stubs were among the litter.

"What's your name?" Aveline asked.

"Julie. Have you come to take me home?"

Lucas knelt beside them. "Why do you need to be rescued, Julie?"

"You don't know?" The *kind* looked from one to the other. "It's got to be on the news. Daddy wouldn't be quiet about what's happened."

"What's happened?" asked Aveline as she shared a concerned glance with Lucas.

The girl said, as if it were the most normal thing in the world, "I've been kidnapped. Are you here to take me home?"

Chapter Two

❧

Sucking in a deep breath, Lucas stared at the *kind* while Aveline asked the youngster if she was okay.

The girl nodded.

"Are you hurt?" he asked.

This time, the girl shook her head.

Aveline put her hand on his arm and motioned with her eyes for him to stand when she did. Telling Julie to gather her things, Aveline kept looking at the girl as she moved several steps away with Lucas.

"Kidnapped?" she murmured, not wanting Julie to overhear. "I've never heard of such a thing in Prince Edward Island."

"I may have." A thought niggled. "There was talk the last time I was in Shushan about a girl going missing from an upscale community north of here. Her family is wealthy, and they're offering a big reward for her return."

"When was that?"

"At least two days ago. Maybe three." He frowned at the mess in the small clearing. "She must have been here all that time."

"But not alone."

As if in response to Aveline, distant crashing echoed through the bushes.

Lucas turned to Julie. "Who was here with you?"

"A man. I don't know his name." She shuddered so hard, he should have been able to hear her bones rattle. When Aveline put an arm around her slender shoulders, the girl leaned on her. "He wanted me to go to a fishing camp. I wouldn't go. He tried to make me, but I bit him." Her face screwed up. "That was yucky, but after that he never said anything to me except when he told me to be quiet or he'd hurt me."

"Does he have a weapon?" Lucas's fingers curled around the rope.

"He has a knife." She shivered. "A big one he wears on his belt."

"A gun?"

She shook her head. "Not that I saw."

More noise split the quiet. When the girl hid her face against Aveline, he said, "Take her to the road and flag down someone. Call the RCMP, and get their help."

"Where are you going?"

"If I tell you I'm going to find your calf, it's not a complete lie." He paused then said, "There's thrashing over there." He pointed in the direction of the marsh. "Could be your calf."

"Or a kidnapper."

He frowned. "You heard him take off like hounds were on his heels when he heard us coming." He turned to leave, hesitated, looked at the girl. "You know what he looks like, ain't so, Julie?"

"He's almost as tall as you, but his head is shaved. He has a black beard, or the beginnings of one." Her nose wrinkled. "He smells bad. Really, really bad."

"If you see anyone like that, Aveline—"

"Or smell him," she interrupted with a wavering smile.

She was trying to make the girl think everything was going to be fine, and he struggled to find a grin of his own. "See or smell him, either way, make yourself scarce. You don't want to confront him on your own."

"I don't," Aveline agreed before holding her hand out to Julie. The girl seized it and clung to Aveline like a possum to its parent. "Let's get going, Julie. Ready?"

"Yes! Don't worry. Daddy will contemplate you."

That comment halted Lucas and Aveline in midstep. "What do you mean?" he asked.

"He'll have a reward for my return, so he'll contemplate you."

"Compensate?" he guessed, trying not to smile but grateful for the levity amid the horror.

"I guess so." Julie shrugged, then swayed.

"Can you walk?" Aveline asked, her concern blaring through the question.

"I think so." She didn't sound sure, so Aveline kept her arm circling the *kind* as they moved around the lower end of the downed trees.

Lucas watched for a moment, wondering if he should have gone with them. No, he had a job to do. Catch the calf…or whatever was making that racket. Aveline and Julie would be safe once the police arrived. He hoped it would be Constable Boulanger, who patrolled the peninsula between Shushan Bay and the Brudenell River. The constable was a *gut* man who'd helped his family before.

He turned in the other direction, pausing every few steps to use his ears to search. There! To the right and ahead of him. He smiled when he saw broken bushes. If Moobeam had come this way, the foolish calf was headed in the worst possible direction. He didn't have a minute to waste.

Waving away a cloud of mosquitos whining around his ears, he went along the faint path the calf had left. It wasn't wide, and he realized he had no idea how old the water buffalo was.

Then he broke free of the trees. Ahead of him was a field of grasses waving with the currents hidden among their stalks. Sunlight glittered on crooked fingers of open water, threatening to blind him. The familiar guilt exploded inside him as he thought how his brother Juan had lost his sight earlier in the year after an antique steam tractor had exploded. Every minute of the days afterward was ultra clear in Lucas's mind. Too many if-onlys had plagued him until Juan's sight had begun to return.

"If I hadn't insisted on you coming with me to Prince Edward Island, this wouldn't have happened," Lucas could remember saying a few weeks after the accident almost four months ago.

"Don't blame yourself." His brother's voice had been calm as they'd sat at the kitchen table in Juan's house.

"But—"

"No! I've got enough guilt already." Juan had been insistent. "I don't need you thinking you played a part in what happened. You never worked on the tractor with me."

"I had an excuse each time you asked me to help."

"So you're excused from feeling guilty."

If it were that easy…

If he hadn't asked Juan to come to Prince Edward Island with him…

If he'd helped…

If he hadn't been so desperate to ignore the past that he'd been oblivious—

Something moved in the marsh, jerking Lucas to the present. He shaded his eyes and gasped when he saw something among the grasses.

Not something. Someone! A man sunk to his knees in the marsh. His shaved head and the beard that shadowed his rough face identified him as Julie's kidnapper. The reek from the rotting vegetation at the bottom of the marsh disguised his odor.

The man's eyes widened in horror as Lucas pushed his way out of the bushes. He tried to move away, but he was stuck. "Hey, man! Let's talk before you do something you'll regret."

"Me? I didn't kidnap a young girl."

"I didn't do her any harm." His gaze ricocheted between Lucas's face and his hands. "I was doing a favor for a friend. I didn't hurt her."

"You scared her half to death. That's crime enough."

The man put his hands to his neck and Lucas realized he thought Lucas was going to use the rope to hang him right then and there. The man didn't know about the Amish belief in nonviolence. Not that Lucas wanted to be judge and jury. He just wanted to make sure the man didn't find a way to slither off like a snake before the cops arrested him.

Walking forward, Lucas halted when his boots started to sink through the grass mat into the water. He didn't want to get stuck, too. Had Aveline and the *kind* found their way to the road? Aveline had seemed capable enough when they'd entered the woods. On the other hand, she'd let her calf escape. Had it been because her thoughts were focused on getting married? He couldn't discount what his cousin Mark had told him about her outrageous flirting.

Had she known about Mark and Kirsten? His conscience warned him he should not be judging others when he didn't have the facts.

"Are you going to stand there and daydream while I'm sinking?" the man jeered.

"You aren't sinking. It's mud, not quicksand." As he tied a loop with the ease of having done it many times with his younger cousin as they'd practiced roping livestock, he asked, "What's your name?"

"I don't have to tell you. You're not a cop." The man bristled, then lost a lot of his bluster when he tried to lift his foot out of the mud and failed.

"No, I'm not." Lucas hefted the rope and swung it a couple of times to test its weight. "I find names make it easier to think of someone else as a person instead of a criminal."

The man chewed on that before saying, "I'm George. George Brudenell."

"Nice try." He played the rope through his fingers, gauging how much it would take to reach the kidnapper. About three meters, he guessed. "We're just up the road from Georgetown, and the Brudenell River is on the other side of the swamp. How about your real name?"

He hung his head. "Trace. My name is Trace Montgomery."

Lucas doubted that was his real name, but said, "Okay, Trace. I'm going to throw this to you."

"You're going to lasso me like a cow?"

"I don't know if I'm that *gut*. I'm aiming to get the rope so you can grab it. Put the loop over your head and around your waist, and I'll pull you in."

"And hand me over to the cops."

"*Ja*, but your other choice is to stay where you are. If you think the mosquitos are bad now, wait until twilight."

Trace waved his hands. "Throw it here."

Lucas started to swing the rope, then let it drop by his side. "One thing you need to know. If you try to tug me in, we'll both be mired."

"I get that."

"*Gut*. So let's start with you throwing your knife away."

He thought Trace would protest but the man pulled a knife from his belt and threw it as far as he could toward the river. A splash was followed by a fountain of water ten meters from him. Trace was strong. Lucas needed to be cautious.

Lucas spun the rope in an easy, smooth rhythm over his head before releasing it. He was shocked when the loop fell over Trace. A quick pull tightened it around the man's waist.

"Hold on to the rope," Lucas yelled. "This isn't going to be fun."

Backing away, he drew the rope around a tree before he began to pull on it. He watched Trace as the rope tightened. Telling him to wiggle his feet out of whatever he had on them, he was surprised when the man shouted he didn't want to leave his boots in the mud.

"Your choice." Lucas started to loosen his grip on the rope. "Stay there with them or get out without them."

Trace cursed Lucas and his ancestors as he tried to free his feet from his boots without toppling into the water. He didn't manage it, and his spewing insults ended with another splash as he smacked face-first into the murky water. At the sound, a pair of ducks launched themselves into the sky.

As soon as Trace had gotten his feet out of his boots, Lucas pulled him toward solid ground. The man tumbled into the water several more times and sputtered mud.

Lucas kept the rope taut, not wanting to let

Trace slip out. When the man was less than a meter from him, he ordered, "Empty your pockets, Trace."

"I don't have anything in them," the other man called. "Nothing except my wallet and a couple of scratch lottery tickets. You can have them if you want. Just get me out of here before I'm eaten alive."

"No, I don't want your things. I want your pockets emptied and turned out."

The man complied, tossing a battered wallet, two lottery tickets and a pack of gum at Lucas's feet.

Lucas shoved them away, then motioned for Trace to step onto the hummock. The man did and reached for the loop around him.

"Don't," Lucas said. "Don't think of it."

The man swore when Lucas wrapped the rope around him a couple times, catching his arms and wrists in the new loops. Lucas tied off the rope, leaving a short length like a leash. It should keep the guy from running away.

"Okay, Trace," he said. "Let's go."

"Where?"

"Where do you think?"

Trace's head dropped lower, and Lucas tightened his grip on the rope and on the man's shoulder.

When Lucas gave him a not-too-gentle shove,

Trace cried, "My tickets! They might be winners."

"I don't think you need to worry about cashing them in."

"I'll need them for bail. If I leave my wallet here, it could get stolen."

Lucas fought the urge to laugh at the criminal worrying about someone stealing from him. On the other hand, the constable would want to see any identification Trace had with him.

As he bent to retrieve the wallet and the tickets, his eyes were caught by a motion. Trace had his bound fists high, a victorious sneer on his face. Before the man could hit him, Lucas skipped to the side, glad he'd left a *gut* length of rope. Unable to stop his forward motion, Trace dropped to his knees.

Before the man could swear again, Lucas said, "I think it'd be better if *you* pick them up."

Trace did and handed them over to Lucas, who shoved the two lottery tickets into Trace's wallet.

Lucas put the wallet next to his own in his pocket. "Let's go," Lucas said. "No more monkey business."

"What are you? A hundred years old?" Trace taunted as he stood. "Nobody says monkey business."

"You're wrong. I do." He gave a quick tug on the rope and another shove to Trace.

It wasn't far to the road, but he doubted it'd be a quick journey while he made sure the other man didn't escape and endanger another *kind*.

Aveline handed the cell phone to the *Englisch* woman who was looking from her to Julie, sitting in Lucas's buggy, with consternation. The woman must have been in her seventies, though she drove a low-slung sports car. Brightly dyed red hair between a garish scarf spilled across her overlarge glasses.

"Did you call the police, young woman?" the woman asked.

"*Ja*." Aveline tried to smile, then gave up.

"What's wrong?"

Not wanting to lie, Aveline said, "A calf has wandered away. We don't want her to get hit by a car. If—"

The woman squinted. "Isn't that the DeSare girl? I saw her picture on the news."

"*Danki*—I mean thank you for letting me use the phone," Aveline replied with a smile. "We need to find our calf."

"She looks like that missing girl."

"Really?" She prayed Julie wouldn't answer.

The *kind* hadn't said a word after they'd reached the road. She'd clung to Aveline, looking back in fear as if she expected her kidnapper to spring out and snatch her. Aveline prayed they'd stay safe and that the sounds they'd heard by the marsh had been made by Moobeam, who was on her way with Lucas.

Julie had relinquished her death grip when Aveline took her to the buggy. The *kind* had crawled in and huddled on the seat while Aveline waved at passing cars. The elderly woman's car had been the first to stop.

Aveline said, "We'll be fine here while we wait for the constable to help us search."

The woman didn't appear to believe her— and why should she when Aveline hadn't told the whole truth?—but nodded and walked to her car. She climbed in, started it and pulled out, heading away from Georgetown. Aveline saw her glance into her rearview mirror.

Going to the buggy, Aveline looked across the road at the trees. What had Lucas found while he'd chased the sounds toward the marsh? Moobeam? She hoped so. How was Aveline going to explain to *Daed* she'd failed to notice a big gap in the fence and had allowed the precious calf to escape?

Thoughts of the wayward calf vanished when Aveline saw Julie curled in a fetal position on the buggy's front seat. The girl was trembling hard, and she had her hands over her face as if she could shut out the world.

Did Lucas keep a blanket in his buggy? Reaching in, Aveline smiled as she pulled out a heavy wool blanket that was too far warm for a July day. She spread it anyways over the girl, who lowered her hands and gazed up without sitting.

"The police are on their way," Aveline said. "They'll get you home."

"Can't you take me?"

"It will be faster with them."

Her face screwed up in distaste. "They'll put me in a dark room with a bright light and inter-rogate me."

"What makes you think that?"

"It's what they do on TV!"

Aveline hoped her smile looked gentle. "I don't watch television, but I know a lot of things on it aren't real."

"Really?"

"*Ja*." She was about to add more but Julie's face lost all color.

The girl squeezed against the driver's side of the buggy, looking like a terrified mouse. A soul-deep cry came from the *kind*. "Don't let him take me! Please, Aveline. Please."

Spinning, Aveline gasped as she saw two forms emerge from the trees. The second was Lucas, who was covered with muck and bits of leaves and twigs. In front of him, secured by a rope, was a disgustingly dirty man who matched the description of Julie's abductor. There was no sign of Moobeam.

What felt like a thousand different emotions erupted through Aveline. Fear, anger, a longing for justice, anxiety about the calf. She pushed the last aside as she stared at the two men. How could Lucas bring that horrible kidnapper to where Julie was?

"He's not going to get near you, *liebling*," Aveline said as she stood in front of the buggy's door. Crossing her arms over her chest, she doubted she looked threatening to the two tall men. If the kidnapper came close, she'd jump into the buggy, give the horse its head and race Julie away.

As Lucas and his prisoner crossed the ditch and reached the road, sirens could be heard in the distance. The man wrapped in the rope tried to escape, but Lucas didn't release his hold. Lucas couldn't move fast enough to avoid the man's bound hands from striking him in the head and knocking him to the ground. The man reached under his shirt and pulled out a switchblade, clicking it open.

"Watch out! He's got a knife!" shrieked Julie from behind her.

Aveline gasped as the man spun to aim the knife at Lucas. Scrambling to his feet, Lucas jumped back. Her own feet propelled her across the road before a single thought formed. Shrieking "No!" she reached to pull Lucas away from the armed man.

Two police cars, their lights flashing and their sirens wailing, appeared around the corner. The man swung his blade as the vehicles skidded to a stop. Lucas backpedaled to escape the downswing of the blade. He tripped and dropped to the ground. The man gave a victorious shout and raised the blade again.

She whirled to evade the man with the knife but didn't make it. A fire seared her left arm before the man fled. He took a pair of steps before two cops tackled him, bringing him down with a loud thump.

Kneeling beside Lucas, she asked, "Are you all right?"

"I'm fine." He stood and wiped mud off his hands. Facing her, he choked on a gasp. "Aveline, you're hurt."

"I am?" Her head seemed light, and she wished someone would blow out the flame scorching her arm. She put her hand up to protect it, then stared at the blood covering her palm.

"Constable!" Lucas shouted as he put his arm around her waist. "We need help! She's been stabbed."

Stabbed? The word seemed alien, floating around her as if it'd been written on a blackboard before disappearing into the heat that grew more fierce with every heartbeat. She closed her eyes, then wished she hadn't as nausea swelled through her.

The world vanished into a kaleidoscope of disconnected images and sensations. Other hands touched her, avoiding the wildfire searing across her upper left arm. Wet poured down it. Why wasn't it dousing the fire?

It felt as if Aveline had blinked only once before her eyes cleared and she realized she was lying in what had to be an ambulance. When had that arrived?

"Julie?" she whispered as thoughts fell through her mind in a landslide. "Where's Moobeam?"

A face appeared above hers. Lucas's! She frowned when she realized she was on her back and he was looking down at her. She moved to sit but gasped as pain exploded up her left arm.

"Stay where you are," he said. "The EMT agreed to let me check on you."

"Where's Julie?"

"She's fine. One of the constables is going to take her to the station so she can be reunited with her folks. She refused to go until she knew you were okay. She's outside and—"

"What happened?"

He took her right hand and tucked it between his. "The guy who kidnapped Julie slashed your left arm with his knife. If you hadn't pushed him away, he would have stabbed me in the chest. You saved my life, Aveline."

"God did. He used me to save you."

"But you were willing to step forward." When she started to retort, he said, "Accept my thanks and get better."

As he turned to go, she grasped his sleeve. "Did they get him?"

"*Ja*." His mouth hardened, and she wondered what had taken place when he'd found the kidnapper in the woods. "He's been arrested for assault and attempted murder." The twinkle returned to his eyes. "Constable Boulanger said there would be more charges after they speak with Julie."

This time, Aveline managed to sit. She swallowed her groan as pain made her light-headed. "Go with her. She's terrified they're going to interrogate her. I should…" She started to swing her legs off the gurney.

A dark-haired woman she didn't recognize stepped forward. She wore an EMT's uniform. "Lie down, Aveline. I've put a temporary bandage on your arm, but we need to get you to the hospital."

"Hospital?" She shook her head. "I can't. Julie—"

"I'll stay with her until her family gets to the

police station," Lucas said. "Just take care of that arm."

"I can't go to the hospital," she repeated, looking from the EMT to Lucas.

"You have to," Lucas said at the same time as the EMT.

"I can't!" Tears, weak tears that embarrassed her, rolled along her face and onto the pillow. "I need to find Moobeam."

The EMT glanced at Lucas, who explained, then said, "Julie's family is already on their way to the police station. I won't be there long. I'll look for Moobeam."

"And bring her home."

"I'll do my best."

She nodded and closed her eyes, hoping his efforts would be enough.

Chapter Three

Aveline heard the door open as she was kneading bread for tomorrow's breakfast. It wasn't easy when her left arm was in a sling. The knife wound hadn't been deep but it had been long, slicing down almost all her upper arm. If she'd moved a few centimeters farther as the kidnapper swung the knife, he would have hit her right in the heart.

"Don't think about it," she told herself as she had each time she'd been woken by a terrifying dream last night. "It's over, *danki*, Lord."

Julie was home with her family, and Lucas had suffered dozens of mosquito bites, but no other damage. Her arm throbbed, but Dr. Armstrong had assured her as he'd stitched the wound closed that she should be able to get rid of the sling in ten days. The criminal whom Lucas had called Trace, though he'd told her it wasn't likely his real name, was behind bars and facing interrogation as charges were being readied against him.

She didn't look forward to having to testify in court. Would she have to? Would she be allowed to? Their bishop, Rodney Wolfe, would make that decision when the time came. Until then, he'd sent word she should focus on healing and thanking God in prayer. The latter she'd done each time last night when she'd woken from another nightmare and found herself in her own room and in her own bed with the familiar sound of her *daed*'s snores coming through the thin walls.

Aveline glanced out the window toward where the water buffalos were gathered by the pond. They were milling about, uneasy with one of their number missing. Her feet itched to propel her out the door. The heavy bandage would protect her arm from the bushes while she searched for Moobeam, and she'd make sure she had plenty of bug spray on.

However, *Daed* and *Mamm* had insisted she stay inside where *Mamm* could keep a close eye on her. Aveline had wanted to argue, but didn't. *Daed* might listen, but debating with *Mamm* would be futile. The process was always the same. Aveline had to admit she was wrong...even when she wasn't; then she had to admit *Mamm* was right...even when she wasn't. Next would come a long lecture about how many mistakes

Aveline had made and how *Mamm* was trying to help her because what man wanted a wife who made so many mistakes? Getting caught tuning out the same old, same old would guarantee the reprimand went on for another fifteen minutes.

Daed's reassurances he'd go into the marsh to look for the missing calf had kept Aveline from sneaking out. Their neighbors would assist, though many of them tried to avoid *Mamm*.

It seemed odd to be in the kitchen alone. Aveline had no idea where *Mamm* had gone. *Mamm*'s happiest place was at her stove, preparing meals for her family. She left the baking to Aveline, and not even stitches should prevent Aveline from having fresh bread ready.

"Anyone home?" called a deep voice.

Looking across the kitchen, she was astonished to see Lucas in the doorway. His bare forearms were scratched and mosquito bites dotted his skin. Mud clung to his boots and trousers, and his suspenders were twisted over his torn shirt.

"What happened to you?" she asked. "Why haven't you changed out of the dirty clothes you wore yesterday?"

"These are different dirty clothes," he replied. Motioning to the back porch, he added, "I can show you faster than I can tell you."

Aveline frowned, troubled by how his eyes glittered with merriment. She'd seen that when he was about to launch a battery of flirting. If she had the nerve, she'd tell him to be on his way, that she didn't have any time or interest in playing his games. If *Mamm* caught wind of how Lucas had paid attention to her, matchmaking would go into highest gear.

Yet she couldn't restrain her curiosity. Wiping sticky dough off her hand the best she could, Aveline hurried to the door where Lucas waited with unexpected patience. Usually he was bouncing from one thing to the next, pausing only to flirt. If he thought she wanted him to lather her with compliments and insincere smiles, he was wrong. His smile seemed genuine, however, when he stepped aside to let her out onto the porch.

"I assume that's your missing calf," he said. "There aren't many water buffalo on the Island."

She stared in shock across the yard. It *was* Moobeam. Her stubby horns and the lighter gray circles around her eyes made identification easy. She was the smallest of the herd, as Aveline was the smallest in her family. Maybe that's why they'd made an instant connection in the hours after Moobeam was born.

Running across the yard, she staggered. Lucas's strong arms caught her before she could hit the grass. She winced when her left arm burned as if she were being stabbed again, but a soft moo from the calf freed her from the sticky webs of pain.

She held out her hand to the calf as she said, "Treat-treat-treat, Moobeam. Don't you want a treat-treat-treat?"

Moobeam regarded her fingers with luminous brown eyes and shook her head hard. Realizing the calf wasn't fooled by her empty hand, Aveline fished in her pocket. She always carried an alfalfa cube or two with her. The cubes of compressed greens were about five centimeters on each side. Her pocket was empty.

"Here," Lucas said.

She looked to see he was holding a handful of green cubes out to her.

"*Danki*," she said, taking the alfalfa cube. "Have you given her others?"

"One, though she let me know she would have enjoyed more."

"They're her favorite." She set the cube on her palm and moved toward the calf, who was watching them with the same leery expression Julie had worn yesterday. She began to croon to the calf. "Moobeam, that's my *gut* girl. Would you like a treat? Treat-treat-treat!"

Aveline wasn't sure if the calf understood the words or smelled the alfalfa, but Moobeam rushed forward. Jumping out of the calf's way, Aveline winced when she jarred her arm. She held out her hand as the calf turned like a bull readying itself to face the matador.

"Watch out!" Lucas shouted, reaching out to her.

"It's okay." Aveline waved him away. "Gently, Moobeam," she murmured as she balanced the cube on her hand where the calf could see it. "*Gut* things for *gut* girls. Treat-treat-treat." When the calf, whose head was level with Aveline's, swept out her tongue to capture the cube, Aveline patted her before running her hand along the animal, checking for injuries.

"I thought she was going to run you down."

She shook her head as she continued examining the calf. "She gets overly excited sometimes, but that's because she's young. I always make sure I'm on the other side of the fence if I give her one of these when she's in the field. She's run smack into it. I wasn't sure if the fence would stay up, and she was smaller then. She's learned not to run into it or into the barn door. She knocked it down one time."

"She's determined, ain't so?"

Smiling, she added, "She's learning to be patient. I hope she didn't get hurt."

"She's fine," Lucas said as he came to stand on the other side of the animal. "Better than the two of us, I daresay."

"I'm glad to hear that." She rested her uninjured elbow on the calf. "Where did you find her?"

"In the pen with my goats. I think they've adopted her as one of their own."

She appraised him anew. "You look like you've been through the swamp."

"Moobeam was tired of being dirty." He brushed his hands against his shirt. "She decided I'd make the best place to wipe off the mire and muck."

"Let me launder and repair them for you."

He waved aside her words. "No need. I've got others as filthy at home. My animals are as eager to rub off their dirt as Moobeam is. She looks okay, ain't so?"

Aveline ran her hands over the calf again and smiled. "She looks great. *Danki*, Lucas, for bringing her home. I thought I might never see her again. We need to let *Daed* know she's been found."

"I saw him on my way here. He asked me to let you know he's running into Shushan to get what he needs to fix the fence. He suggested you keep this wandering girl in the barn until he's done."

"A *gut* idea. *Danki*, Lucas."

"You don't need to keep saying that."

"Saying what?"

"'*Danki*, Lucas.' I know you're glad to have the calf, but you saved my life yesterday, and I thanked you once. You're making me feel ungrateful."

Before Aveline could answer, she heard *Mamm* say, "You should be grateful, Lucas Kuepfer."

Aveline bit her lip as Lucas's face shuttered. Lucas and his family were close, and when *Mamm* had bad-mouthed his cousin Mark, she'd insulted all of them. That the whole situation had been Aveline's fault hadn't lessened the sharpness of *Mamm*'s tongue.

Chalonna Lampel wasn't a woman who would allow anyone to ignore her. She was almost as tall as Lucas and as broad as she was tall. Not a hint of gray dared to mar her blonde hair or a wrinkle form in her dress or apron. It wasn't her immaculate appearance or her size that commanded attention. It was her assumption she knew best what others should do. Aveline had asked *Daed* why he'd married *Mamm* when he was so laid-back. His reply had been a trite, "Opposites attract."

A wide smile tilted *Mamm*'s lips. "I didn't know you were here," she said as if Lucas visited every day. Her voice became warm, a sure sign she had matchmaking on the mind.

"*Mamm*," Aveline replied, wanting to put an end to *Mamm*'s plans before they started, "he brought Moobeam back."

"Moobeam?" *Mamm* gave a soft laugh. "A silly name, ain't so?"

"*Mamm*—"

"Let the man get a word in edgewise, Aveline. No one appreciates a woman who's a chatterbox. How many times have I told you to make every word count?"

Heat coursed up her face, and Aveline knew she was blushing. Not at the reprimand. She'd been given enough of those throughout her life. She no longer reacted to the *Mamm*-isms that always sounded like platitudes.

Not heeding her own advice, *Mamm* kept up a steady chatter as she insisted Lucas come into the house. "You look like you could use a *gut* hot cup of *kaffi*," she announced before telling Aveline to take care of the calf.

Aveline bit her lip so she didn't retort there was no need to remind her what she should do. She wasn't a *kind* any longer. She pushed her frustration aside as *Mamm* herded Lucas into the kitchen as if he were a lamb and she the ever-watchful sheepdog.

Being upset at *Mamm* wouldn't gain Aveline anything but vexation, and she should be thanking God for Moobeam's return. She put a hand on the calf's right horn before moving her toward the barn. Moobeam paused when she saw where they were headed. The calf must be missing her own *mamm* and the rest of the herd, but *Daed* was right. If Moobeam was put in the field with the others, she would sneak out again. This time she could get hurt instead of finding goats for playmates.

The green alfalfa cubes convinced Moobeam to follow Aveline into the barn where the whole herd would spend the upcoming cold months. Putting the calf into a pen, Aveline rubbed the water buffalo's nose. Moobeam made an appreciative snuffling sound.

Though she would have preferred to remain in the barn and avoid another bout of *Mamm*'s less than subtle matchmaking, she couldn't leave Lucas to face it alone. He'd done her a great favor by bringing Moobeam home. The best way to repay him would be to help him evade playing a part in one of *Mamm*'s matchmaking schemes.

When Aveline opened the kitchen door, she wasn't surprised to see Lucas standing next to it. He must be trying to find a way to excuse himself as *Mamm* fussed over him while apologizing for the mess Aveline had made. It wasn't a mess. Just flour and dough where she'd done her best to knead the bread with one hand.

"Do *komm* in, Lucas, and sit down," *Mamm* ordered in what Aveline called her la-di-da voice, the one she assumed when she had company she intended to impress. "Enjoy some *kaffi* while I get you some cake."

"Sorry," Aveline said out of the corner of her mouth. "She gets like this."

"It's no problem." His reply was polite but wasn't true. He kept glancing at the clock on the light blue wall behind the sink. Either he had to be somewhere and he was late, or he wanted to flee.

She tried to edge past Lucas when *Mamm* motioned for her to get a small plate from the cupboard. She bumped her injured arm. When she couldn't swallow her yelp of pain, he faced her.

"I'm sorry," he said. "I didn't give you enough room and you've hurt yourself."

"I should have watched where I was going." She almost gave him a reassuring smile.

Mamm was watching them like a hawk eyeing a mouse. She'd pounce if either Aveline or Lucas offered the slightest sign they had feelings—even pity or guilt—for each other. Then she realized it didn't matter. *Mamm* was already imagining her standing beside Lucas as they spoke their wedding vows in the presence of the whole community.

That was confirmed when *Mamm* smiled. "Don't you two look—"

A loud rap on the front door interrupted her. Who was knocking there? They didn't have a lot of visitors. Her *mamm*'s sharp tongue had ensured that.

"I'll get it," Aveline said, glad for a reason to put some distance between her and the tension she could feel radiating off Lucas.

Rushing across the large living room, she

threw open the door. An *Englischer* stood on the other side. He was older than she was by a decade, and her inexperienced eyes could tell his dark suit was expensive. His black shoes shone from a polishing.

"Can I help you?" she asked as she pulled her gaze from those bright shoes to the man's stern face. She heard footsteps behind her. Not just *Mamm*'s but Lucas's.

"I'm Philip DeSare," the man said. "Are you Aveline Lampel?"

"I am." She saw two cars, then another turn into their farm lane. Cars often turned around there, but she'd never seen so many at once. Focusing her attention on the man at the door, she asked, "How can I help you, Mr. DeSare?"

"You've already helped me, Miss Lampel." He gave her a smile, his white teeth bright in his tanned face. Not tanned from long hours of working in the sun, she guessed when she saw his manicured hands.

"I have?"

"I'm Julie DeSare's father. I've come to thank you for saving her life."

Lucas could see that Aveline was at a loss for words as she stared at the *Englischer* in the doorway. Why not? He got choked up thinking of the girl and the fear she must have experienced with Trace...or whatever his name was.

It was Chalonna who broke the silence. "My daughter saved your daughter's life? What are you talking about?"

Mr. DeSare's smile didn't waver as he turned from Aveline to Chalonna. "You must be proud of her, Mrs. Lampel. If not for your daughter and the man who was with her—Lucas Kuepfer—"

"Aveline and Lucas? The two of them were together when they rescued your daughter?" Chalonna latched on to that one fact out of everything the *Englischer* had said.

Lucas should have expected that response, but he was shocked that Chalonna was focusing on Aveline and him rather than on Julie. Seeing the speculation in Aveline's *mamm*'s eyes, he knew the sooner he put an end to the conversation, the better. It'd be simpler to jump in and say what he must if his head wasn't throbbing. Julie's abductor had hit him hard before reaching for his knife.

"By chance," he said. "We ran into each other. Almost literally."

The other man was confused because he asked, "Are you Lucas Kuepfer?"

"I am."

Mr. DeSare's smile broadened. "I'm glad I've got the opportunity to thank both of you. As I was saying, if it wasn't for the two of you, my daughter might still be in the hands of the beast who kidnapped her."

Chalonna's eyes grew large, and Lucas realized the gravity of what had happened yesterday was at last creeping past her matchmaking instincts. "Are you saying my daughter helped your daughter escape a kidnapper?"

"She and Mr. Kuepfer did." Mr. DeSare looked puzzled. "How did you think Miss Lampel was injured?"

"She told me," Aveline's *mamm* said with a frown, "that happened while she searched for a calf."

"I didn't lie, *Mamm*," she said. "I didn't want to upset you with the details."

"Hmm…" was all Chalonna said before she invited the *Englischer* in and urged him to sit. She bustled away to get him *kaffi* and the piece of the cake she'd already cut.

Lucas heard Aveline release an unsteady breath and wondered what it would be like to live in a house with her domineering *mamm*. An unkind thought, he reminded himself as the *Englischer* sat on the sofa.

Aveline chose one of a pair of rocking chairs facing the couch. "How is Julie doing, Mr. DeSare?"

"She seems to be doing far better than I expected, but she refuses to talk about what happened. Not to me, not to the police. I'm not sure why."

"I do." Her lips tilted in a gentle smile. "She believes she's going to be harshly interrogated as she's seen on some program on the television."

Mr. DeSare sighed. "I've told our housekeeper not to watch those shows when Julie is around. It's too much for a nine-year-old."

"She's nine?" Lucas asked as he sat on the other end of the sofa. "I'd guessed from how well she spoke that she's eleven or twelve."

"She's tall for her age and precocious. It comes from being an only child. She's been alone a lot since her mother died when Julie was three." He reached under his coat and drew out two slips of paper. "Anyhow, I wanted to deliver these in person so I could thank you face-to-face." He handed one to Lucas, then stretched to give the other to Aveline.

Lucas looked down at what he held and gasped. It was a check for twelve thousand, five hundred dollars. "What is this?"

"Your half of the reward I announced for the return of my daughter," Mr. DeSare said with a smile.

"We can't accept this." Aveline held her check out to the *Englischer*. "God put us in the right spot at the right time. We were His hands. Our reward is knowing we were able to help."

"Exactly," Lucas said, offering his own check to Mr. DeSare. "We're grateful for your generosity, but we can't accept."

The *Englischer* stood. "I won't take back the checks. I announced the reward the day the incident began. You two earned it, and besides, I'm not someone who reneges on my word. That's not how I do business."

Coming to his feet, Lucas said, "We must not—"

He was amazed when Aveline interrupted him by saying, "I'm sure we can work out something, Mr. DeSare. Would it be possible for you to meet with our bishop, Rodney Wolfe?"

"If you believe it's necessary, of course, I will." His mouth worked and, for the first time, he lost his polished veneer. "I want to repay a debt that can never be repaid."

"I'm glad we were there when Julie needed us," Aveline said.

Mr. DeSare handed her a business card. "Here's my number. Call when you can set up the meeting with your bishop." He hesitated. "You do have a phone, don't you?"

"*Ja*," she replied. "But it's only for emergencies."

Though he seemed nonplussed, he said, "All right. I'll check back with you in a few days, if that's okay?"

Lucas answered, "We'll let you know when the meeting is set."

The *Englischer* nodded to her and then to Lucas as Chalonna returned from the kitchen. With another nod, he started to turn toward the door.

It crashed open before he could touch the knob. A wave of noise washed into the house along with a single person.

Elam Lampel, Aveline's *daed*, was a lanky man. His bushy, graying beard reached to the second button on his light green shirt. His eyes were the same deep green as his daughter's, and they were almost popping out of his head as he slammed the door behind him.

"I don't know what's going on out in the yard," Elam said, panting as if he'd run a marathon. "There must be twenty people out there, and every last one of them is acting as if they've lost their minds. Shouting questions at me and trying to take my picture and sticking microphones in my face." He noticed Mr. DeSare for the first time. "Who are you?"

"Philip DeSare. I came to thank your daughter for saving mine."

"Did you bring that crowd with you?"

He shook his head. "No, but I'm responsible for them, I'm afraid." He looked out the window and scowled. "Reporters. Chasing the story of

Julie's kidnapping and rescue. Do you have a back door?"

"*Ja*," Aveline said. "But there's only way to the road."

With a sigh, Mr. DeSare sat again. "If you don't mind, Mrs. Lampel, I'll have that *kaffi* now." He took out a cell phone. "It may take the constable a while to get here and persuade the reporters to leave. They've been loitering around my house, and they followed me here."

Lucas lowered the shades while Aveline walked into the kitchen. By the time he'd joined her there, leaving Mr. DeSare to explain to her *daed* why he was there, she was struggling to knead the bread she'd been making.

She looked up when he came into the kitchen but said nothing. She didn't have to. Her grim expression warned her thoughts matched his own. Their lives had changed today, and neither could guess when they'd return to normal.

Or if.

Chapter Four

It was an hour before Lucas was able to return to his farm more than two kilometers from the Lampel place. He was amazed how stubborn the reporters had been when a pair of constables had arrived to ask them to leave the Lampels and their guests alone. Several had argued, insisting they would leave as soon as he and Aveline and Mr. DeSare answered a few questions.

Aveline had shaken her head in horror at the idea of confronting the press, and his own stomach had tightened. Mr. DeSare, who'd never raised his voice when he went out on the porch to confer with Constable Boulanger and the other officer whose name Lucas hadn't caught, had made it clear if the reporters didn't disperse as the police had asked, there would be dire consequences.

Mr. DeSare hadn't explained further, but the looks exchanged among the reporters gathered in the Lampels' front yard told Lucas they were in awe of Julie's *daed*. They returned to their cars and began to leave. It wasn't quick because the cars had been left in a tangle, parked every which way.

The biggest shock had been when one of the police cars began to follow Lucas as he'd walked along the road to his own farm. It had stopped at the end of his lane while he'd headed for the house and collection of barns and outbuildings edged by his potato fields.

Lucas had glanced over his shoulder in time to discover a trio of cars parking along the main road behind the constable's car. Another vehicle drove slowly past, the driver's head turning to keep an eye on the lane. The reporters were persistent. On one hand, he had to admire their determination to do their jobs, but he wished they would find someone else to focus on.

He grimaced. They had. Aveline and the De-Sares were also in their sights. How could the search for a wayward calf have become such a circus?

Pausing in midstep, he peered at his brother's farm next door. A slight rise concealed the single-story house, but he could see the barn's roof. Would the press bother his family if he didn't answer their questions?

He loped toward the road. He needed to warn Juan and his family they might be in reporters' sights. When he waved, the constable in the car at the end of the lane rolled down his window.

"Everything okay, Lucas?" the cop asked.

"Fine. Just need to check on something with my brother." He was hedging, he knew, but he didn't want a police escort. He ignored the cramp in his gut as he wondered what he'd say if Aveline or Mr. DeSare's daughter asserted the same thing. Wouldn't he have been the first to caution that would be unwise?

He slipped among the trees along the road when he saw several cars moving in his direction. Reaching the farm where Juan lived with his wife, Annalise, and her daughter and her late husband's *grossmammi* and two dogs, he edged around the barn where his sister-in-law kept her woodworking tools and headed for the white farmhouse. His eyes caught a motion near the road. Reporters? Or a member of his family? He'd face the former to protect the latter.

The scent of fresh lemons caught his attention as he crossed the yard. It was, he realized, coming from his blonde sister-in-law Annalise. Had she been making something with lemons or using a lemon-scented polish in her woodworking shop? He started to call to her, then rushed forward as a car stopped in front of the small display stand Annalise kept near the road. She filled it with small items she'd made in her shop. Tourists often stopped and admired her crafts. She left an honor box for payment every day but Sunday when she draped a tarpaulin over the stand to signal no business could be done on the Sabbath.

Annalise smiled in his direction before turning to greet the three people getting out of the car. The woman wore a bright red dress and had her hair in a messy ponytail. She shrugged on a cream-colored coat and checked something on its lapel. A man who looked as if he'd slept in his clothes for the past month adjusted his tie and tried to smooth the wrinkles out of his shirt. A third person, whom Lucas thought at first was a young man because of close-cropped hair dyed an unnatural shade of red on one side and pure white on the other, balanced a heavy camera on one shoulder. Then the camera carrier called out to the others in a woman's voice.

"If I stand here," the camera woman said, "I can get the stand and the house in the background."

"Good!" the woman in the red dress replied. "Gordie, don't get in my shot."

The man frowned as he pulled a notepad from his pocket and flipped it open. "You don't need to remind me every time we get out of the car. Give it a rest, Maggie."

As they scowled at each other, Lucas bent toward Annalise and whispered, "Don't answer their questions."

"What do you mean?" she asked.

"I'll explain after they go."

Gordie surged forward. "Are you Lucas Kuepfer's sister-in-law?"

Annalise looked at Lucas, then said, "I'm sorry. I can't talk now. I've got bread in the oven, and I don't want it to burn."

As she turned to leave, Gordie stepped in front of her. "I won't keep you."

Before Annalise could reply, Lucas said, "You heard her. She can't talk now."

"Who are you?" the woman called Maggie asked.

Thanking God that Constable Boulanger had been able to sneak them unseen out the Lampels' back door, he smiled. "A concerned neighbor who wanted to let her know you've got cameras."

When Annalise looked at him in amazement, he gave a slight shake of his head as if brushing aside a bug. She turned away, and he guessed she didn't want the *Englischers* to see her grin.

"It isn't our way to have our pictures taken," he went on when nobody else spoke, "so turn that camera off."

The woman holding the camera swung it down from her shoulder. "Sorry. I didn't know that." She fired a glare at the female reporter. "It might have been nice if someone had told me that."

Maggie shrugged in indifference. Her nose

wrinkled, and he guessed he reeked from chasing Moobeam around the goat pen. He wasn't going to apologize for being a farmer.

"Will you do as she asked and excuse us?" he asked when the reporters didn't go to their car. Motioning for Annalise to follow, he took a single step toward the house before Maggie called out.

"Wait a minute," she said. "We want to buy some of…" She glanced at the stand for the first time. "These little wooden thingamajigs."

"Choose which one you want," Annalise replied, "and put the payment in the metal box."

"Did Lucas make them?" asked Gordie.

"No."

Annalise became silent as the woman and the man each selected a small boat. The woman glanced at Annalise, then grabbed several other items. Hiding his smile, he wondered if the reporter thought she could bribe Annalise into blabbing about him.

As he and Annalise walked to the rear porch, Lucas didn't look back. It might have been amusing to see the reporters' expressions, but they could have seen the motion as an invitation to continue the uncomfortable conversation.

As soon as they were out of earshot of the reporters, Lucas said, "*Danki* for not using my name."

"You introduce yourself right away to strangers. When you didn't, I assumed something wasn't right. What's going on?"

He glanced at the fields surrounding the house. "Where's my brother gotten to?"

"Juan drove into Shushan to get a part he needs for the potato harvester."

"An easy fix?"

"He thinks so. You know he'll let you know if he needs any help." She faced him. "What's going on, Lucas? Why didn't you want those people to know your name?"

"Any chance you have lemonade and I can explain over a glass?"

"Sounds like a *gut* idea." Her eyes widened. "What's going on?"

He turned to see another car slowing to a stop. A camera was aimed out the window, and he grasped her arm and pulled her around the corner of the house. Neither of them slowed as shouts came from behind them.

"This story had better be *gut*," Annalise said in a grim tone.

"I don't know about *gut*, but it is quite a story." *And far from over.*

"You look deep in thought."

"I am, Valetta." Aveline raised her eyes, shifting in her chair at the kitchen table. She bit back a groan as she moved her injured arm. Cupping her elbow in her other hand, she forced a smile.

Valetta Whetstone had been her dearest friend since Valetta's family had arrived on the Island shortly after the Lampels. When she and Aveline's brother, Wes, started walking out together, Aveline had been delighted. She couldn't imagine anyone better than her friend to steady her brother's impulsive ways. Valetta was of medium height with medium brown hair and a medium temperament. Aveline had never seen her friend get hot under the collar or give someone a cold shoulder. Valetta seemed wired to a center of calm, drawing others into her peace. In the six months since Valetta had confided Wes had first offered her a ride home in his buggy, Aveline had seen a *wunderbaar* change in her brother. He no longer seemed to flare in anger each time *Daed* or *Mamm* made a suggestion to him.

Aveline wished her friend could offer her the same serenity while they enjoyed a cup of tea and the raisin-peanut-chocolate-chip cookies Valetta had brought with her. Aveline needed some tranquility because the day had taken so many unexpected turns. A *wunderbaar* one like Moobeam being found safe. An unsettling one like the swarm of reporters imprisoning her in her own home. But the most unsettling had been when Mr. DeSare had pulled out two checks and presented them to her and Lucas.

Her first reaction had been thinking—for the length of a single heartbeat—how that money could help build their herd. She'd silenced that thought instantly, but felt guilty it'd formed. If Lucas or her family had any idea, they would have every right to be ashamed of her. She was glad she'd heeded *Daed*'s advice to think all she spoke, but to not speak all she thought.

"What's on your mind?" Valetta asked then laughed. "As if I didn't know. It isn't a what, but a who. Your *mamm* met me at the door and told me Lucas Kuepfer called on you this morning."

Aveline resisted the urge to roll her eyes. Trust *Mamm* to take the facts and weave them into such a reality that had little to do with what had happened but was laced with enough truth so nobody could accuse her of lying.

"Lucas found Moobeam with his goats and brought her home." Aveline smiled. Getting upset over *Mamm*'s matchmaking was silly. *Mamm* wasn't going to change.

"And stayed for a couple of hours."

She leaned forward, being careful not to bump her stitches. Lowering her voice, she explained to her friend what had occurred. "As you can see, he was avoiding having to talk to the media."

"You're going to have to talk to them sooner or later."

"Mr. DeSare said we wouldn't have to."

"He doesn't control the press." Valetta took a sip of her tea. "They're chasing a story, and I doubt they'll stop until they get it."

"I'm not going to talk to them." She shuddered.

"Let Lucas talk to them. He likes to talk to everyone. You can drop him in the midst of a crowd of strangers, and he'll find something to talk about in ten seconds. Give him a minute, and he'll be flirting with a woman." Her eyes sparkled. "I'm assuming he flirted with you while he was here."

"I didn't pay attention."

Valetta sat straighter. "How could you not pay attention when a *gut*-looking guy like Lucas is flirting with you?"

"You're beginning to sound like *Mamm*."

"She wants you to be happy, Aveline." Valetta's tone remained even. "Wes says she wants her *kinder* happy and secure."

Shaking her head, Aveline picked up her teacup before she said something she might regret. *Mamm* wanted to show the whole world she'd done an excellent job with her *kinder*. Her proof would be found by seeing each of them settled in marriage. Or would she be satisfied with that?

Would she push for *kins-kinder* to show she was an excellent *grossmammi*?

Would anything Aveline and her brothers did be enough?

"You need," Valetta said, "to cut your *mamm* some slack."

"I've tried." She waved aside her friend's response. "No need to tell me I sound like a whining preteen."

"You don't whine, Aveline. Not once have I heard you say anything about how you didn't want to move here." Valetta's smile was tinged with sorrow. "Don't worry. I won't ask. I've seen how withdrawn you become when your family talks about planning to relocate here. They've got stories. You sit and say nothing."

Shocked her friend had discerned what Aveline had believed was hidden, she said, "I think you're wrong about Lucas."

"So we're going to talk about him again?"

"I just wanted to say chatting with plain folks isn't the same as facing the press. I'm glad Mr. DeSare was able to convince them to leave." She frowned. "Though I don't know how he was able to do that when they ignored the constables."

Valetta folded her arms on the table. "Rumors say Philip DeSare, the CEO of DeSare Industries, which is a big, big, big company, is going to be appointed to a post in the national government."

"Where did you hear that?" she asked, eager to change the subject.

"From your brother. Wes is fascinated with politics, and he follows provincial and national news."

"Does he still have his portable radio? *Mamm* was furious when she found it, and she ordered him to get it out of the barn. He didn't heed her for months, then told *Daed* he was donating it to a thrift shop last year when…"

"When he got serious about us?"

"*Ja*. Did you convince him to get rid of it?"

"Not exactly." Valetta's smile softened as her gaze turned inward.

Toward her heart, Aveline guessed, feeling a pinch of envy. Had her own gaze ever looked so happy when she'd been walking out with Merle?

She was glad when her friend went on, halting her own uncomfortable thoughts. "We talked about how the radio was a point of contention between him and your parents. He came to see starting our married life with a disagreement with your *daed* and *mamm* hanging over his head wasn't the best idea. He gave the radio away and began reading newspapers." She took another sip of her tea. "Anyhow, Philip DeSare has been in the news a lot lately."

"Are you saying the reporters didn't want to

annoy Mr. DeSare so he wouldn't talk to them if he got that appointment?"

"Exactly."

"I wonder if he'll change his mind about taking such a position after what happened to Julie."

Valetta shook her head. "You're wondering about the wrong thing, Aveline."

"What do you mean?"

"You shouldn't be wondering about whether he'll take the job. You should be wondering if that job had anything to do with Julie's abduction."

Chapter Five

Lucas stepped out of his barn as Aveline raced toward him, waving one hand over her head to get his attention. She wasn't wearing the sling. Had she gotten her stitches out already? No, they needed to remain in at least ten days, and it'd been only five since they'd found Julie DeSare huddled by the broken trees.

"Is she here?" Aveline called.

"She? She who?" he shouted, then trotted to her. He glanced back at the potato harvester he'd been checking. Half of the thin metal arms that dug into the hills to excavate the potatoes were bent, though he'd straightened them after the last harvest. How had they gotten twisted? He'd been careful not to toss anything, not even a horse blanket, on them since last year.

"Moobeam!"

"She got out again?" He halted and scanned the barnyard.

Sure enough. There, beyond the yard where he kept his goats, the water buffalo calf had its big head over the fence, sniffing at the smaller animals. Some goats were curious about the calf. Others paid her no attention.

"She's here," he yelled.

Aveline ran to the far side of the goats' pen. Looping a rope around the compliant calf's head, she led Moobeam to where Lucas was walking up to her. Instead of the smile he'd expected to see, her face was grim.

Looking past her in the direction of the road, which was empty of slow-moving cars prowling to catch sight of him, he asked, "How did you get here without your paparazzi?"

"Mine? I thought they were camping out here."

"They try, but they get moved along pretty quickly by the cops. Have they been bothering you?"

"Not as much as they bother *Mamm*. She doesn't like the fact that nobody is visiting because they don't want to run the gauntlet."

He nodded, guessing what she didn't say. Chalonna was frustrated no young men had paid a call on Aveline. A surprising pinch of something distasteful twisted in his gut as he thought of other men paying the pretty redhead attention. Had he bumped his head harder than he'd thought when Trace attacked him? He couldn't figure out any other reason why Aveline walking out with someone else would bother him. Or, he didn't want to figure it out.

Escaping the vicious circle of his thoughts, Lucas asked, "How did you give the reporters the slip?"

"By following Moobeam's roundabout trail. She doesn't like the road. The press prefers to stay away from the marsh." Looking at her muddy sneakers, she said, "I don't have much choice but to go and get her when she's out."

"She's gotten out before this? I mean, since we chased through the marsh looking for her."

"*Ja*, twice. Both times, I found her right away. When I couldn't this time, I assumed she came here."

He gave her a jaunty grin but she didn't return it. "Does she want to get more mud on me?"

"Don't flatter yourself. She came to see your goats, not you."

Putting his hand over his heart, he pretended to pout. "Oh, you know how to hit a man right where it hurts."

"I'm sure you'll recover." Her lips remained in a straight line.

Wondering what it would take to get a smile from her, he continued. "Does she think she's a goat? They're escape artists."

"It doesn't take much of an escape artist to

walk out a gate that was left open enough for her to slip through."

"Who was that careless?"

She met his eyes. "It wasn't careless, Lucas. Two stones had been stuck into the ground on either side of the gate, making sure it was open just wide enough for Moobeam to get through, but not the others."

He stared at her, not wanting to believe her tense words. "Who would do something like that?"

"I don't want to accuse anyone, but I've got my suspicions."

He scowled. "The press?"

"Who else would be so foolish to let a valuable animal out? Maybe they think they can catch me trying to catch her."

Shaking his head, he said, "Something doesn't ring true with that. The media are already on thin ice with the authorities. They don't want to spend time sitting in a jail cell. How would a wandering calf help them get their story?"

"I don't know." Misery laced through her words. "You're right, but I don't know who would do such a thing. Moobeam could have been hurt or killed while out on her own."

"Mattie had to deal with vandalism when she first started the farm shop." He grimaced as he thought of the boys who'd gotten his teenage cousin, Daryn, into trouble last year.

"Those kids were put on notice that they'd get more than a warning if they caused more damage. It seems to have worked with them." She glanced at the huge calf beside her. "I should take Moobeam back."

Instead of telling her goodbye, he was shocked to hear himself say, "Something else is bothering you, Aveline. What is it?"

When her green eyes widened, he realized he could easily read her emotions when he had to struggle to recognize his own. Had he buried his feelings so deeply after Robin tossed him aside that he couldn't find them any longer?

"I was planning to come over today," she said so softly he had to strain to hear her, "before I discovered Moobeam was gone."

"Why?"

She shuffled her feet in the dirt. "It can wait."

"Your face says otherwise."

Putting her hand to her cheek that flushed, the color swallowing her freckles, she lowered her eyes. "I don't know how important it is."

"Important enough for you to consider coming over to talk about it." He opened the gate to the goat enclosure. "Put Moobeam in here. That'll make her happy."

Aveline smiled as she did as he suggested and then closed the gate behind the calf. She watched the animals eagerly greet each other.

When she looked at him, he half turned away and waved his arm. "*Komm mol.* We can talk in the equipment shed. I'm checking the potato harvester. You can talk while I'm working."

"As long as you can work and listen at the same time."

"Despite what you've heard, Aveline, my mind doesn't run on a single track. I can multitask." He pulled a hammer out of his belt. "See? I can carry a hammer and walk at the same time. Aren't you impressed with my mental and physical dexterity?"

"I'm impressed with your sarcasm." Her laugh took the sting out of her words. Its lilting warmth delighted him, something he hadn't expected. He'd closed his ears to such sounds since Robin had accused him of being too serious. If anyone had asked, he would have said he was quite the opposite, but the certainty in her voice had shaken him, making him question every opinion he'd believed was ironclad.

Smiling, he put the hammer in his belt and led the way into the barn. He shouldn't have been upset she'd accepted the public perception of him as the whole truth. He'd done the same for her. Not once since they'd met on the road and gone in search for the calf had she acted as if she were interested in anything other than the task at hand.

Of course, he was giving her the chance she

might have been waiting for. They'd be out of view of everyone else while they were in the shed.

Are you afraid to be alone with an attractive woman? Are you afraid she'll persuade you to set aside your determination to show you're fun instead of being serious about something? The thought shook him to his marrow because he wasn't sure of the answer.

He didn't like being uncertain about things. Once he'd believed he knew the life God had mapped out for him. That now seemed like someone else's life. Changing everything about his plans had been simple. Or so he'd thought. Three years after Robin had tossed him aside, he'd come to understand the tiniest change had huge ramifications.

"What happened?" Aveline asked, giving him the opportunity to escape his thoughts.

"To what?" He had the feeling she'd been talking and he'd missed what she'd been saying while stuck in his own thoughts.

"Your harvester." She pointed to the piece of equipment he'd been working on.

"I was working on it when I heard you coming down the lane." He squatted next to where it was parked beside a half wall. "It was fine when I put it away last fall."

"The digger arms look like spaghetti."

"I agree. I would have had to have my eyes

closed not to notice it." Pulling out his hammer, he tapped it against the metal. Enough to straighten it but not so hard he broke the thin strip. "I don't have any idea how this happened. If I hadn't done another check before I tried to use it, the harvester would have been wrecked."

When she didn't answer, he saw her staring over his head at the opposite wall of the shed. He guessed she wasn't thinking about the tools and spare parts he had hanging on the pegboard there. Her gaze shifted to meet his, and he saw dismay and something else in her eyes. Anger? Fear? Annoyance? No, the emotion was far stronger than mere annoyance.

"Lucas, doesn't it strike you as odd?" Her voice was tight when she spoke, as if she were choosing each word after long deliberation. "Doesn't it strike you as odd that on the same day the gate on our field is propped open so a valuable animal had the chance to escape and risk being hurt or killed, you find an important piece of equipment damaged?"

"Coincidence," he said, but his fingers curled around the hammer so hard his nails tried to bite into the wood.

"I wish I could believe you're right, but…"

Setting himself on his feet, he put the hammer on the short wall, half expecting to see his fingerprints pressed into the handle. "What you're suggesting, Aveline, is something I don't want to consider."

"Do you think I want to? I can't ignore what's right in front of me." When she looked from the harvester to the pen where Moobeam was surrounded by the goats, he did the same.

The facts seemed undeniable, but he couldn't be drawn into something that might prove to be nothing more than a bizarre theory. Not that he believed Aveline had suggested it that way. There was enough dubiousness in her voice to reveal she didn't want to believe her own words.

"Who would do such things? And why?" he asked.

A faint smile edged her taut lips. "I knew you'd ask those questions because I'm asking them myself."

"Have you found any answers?"

"None that make sense." She squared her shoulders and looked him straight in the eyes. "But it doesn't make sense, either, that someone let Moobeam out and your harvester has been almost ruined."

Lucas arched his brows. "I'd like to believe it's a coincidence."

"So would I, but I can't."

"Neither can I." He leaned on the half wall. "This isn't what you had on your mind out by the goats. What's bothering you?"

"Valetta came to visit this morning."

"Valetta Whetstone?" He'd heard rumors Valetta was going to be Aveline's sister-in-law, but didn't ask for details. Valetta was also Aveline's *gut* friend, one of the few women who dared to speak her mind to Chalonna, even before she'd started walking out with one of the Lampel brothers. Lucas wasn't sure which one.

"*Ja*." Aveline hesitated then went on. "Valetta said a government appointment Mr. DeSare is supposed to get might have something to do with why Julie was abducted. It's a prestigious job that will give him influence over the Island's future."

"What do you think?"

"I don't know anything about the appointment, but I do know the man who took her seemed desperate."

"Kidnapping is the act of a desperate person. No sane person who could see another alternative would do such a thing."

She wrapped her arms around herself, and he wondered if she believed the motion would hold the evils of the world at bay. Then he imagined how it would be to have his arms around her instead. The top of her head would fit right beneath his chin, and if he tilted his head, he could rest his cheek on the red hair in front of her *kapp*.

"I agree," she said and he shook aside the thoughts he shouldn't be savoring, "but that man didn't seem like someone who did a lot of planning. He grabbed Julie, yet he couldn't get her to go to his fishing hut. He ran away when we approached, not waiting to see if we were armed or—to be honest—if we'd even see Julie. He could have found a way out of the marsh if he'd done any exploring before he'd taken Julie. Wouldn't you have devised an escape route?"

He gave her a wry grin. "I'm kind of hoping I never need one."

"You know what I mean."

"I do, and I can see your point. Trace didn't seem to have anything figured out once he had Julie."

"Do you think," she said, sounding as if she were putting the pieces together in her mind at the same time she was musing aloud, "it's because Trace didn't make the plan? That someone else did?"

He pushed away from the wall. "Do you realize what you're saying?"

Her face lost every bit of color except for her freckles that looked as dark as if she'd been jabbed with a pencil point. "*Ja*. That Trace didn't have the idea of kidnapping Julie, and the person who did is walking around free."

"If that's so, Julie could be in grave danger. Mr. DeSare might not have considered this."

"We need to contact him and share our suspicions." She faltered. "Are you going to contact him?"

"Not directly."

"What do you mean?"

He motioned for her to follow him. "You'll see."

Lucas didn't add anything else as he strode along his farm lane toward the main road. Aveline had to scurry to keep up. When she asked where they were going, he didn't answer. The answer would be apparent.

As if he'd blown a silent dog whistle, when they neared the end of the lane, vans appeared, *Englischers* burst out, rushing toward Aveline and him. Questions were shouted, so mangled with each other, he couldn't understand anything.

Beside him, Aveline seemed to shrink. She stopped and took one step back, then another.

"It's okay," Lucas whispered.

"How can you say—"

A siren gave a short burst as a car stopped across the end of the farm lane. Constable Boulanger was out of his vehicle in seconds. "Back off!" he shouted to the reporters. "You know what you've been told about stepping onto private property."

"We're not on private property," one reporter shouted. "We're on the road."

"Where you're blocking traffic."

Lucas almost laughed. Other than the reporters' vans and the police car, there weren't any vehicles in sight in either direction. He kept his face stern as he waited for the constable to herd the press away from him and Aveline. Within minutes, the vans were turning around and driving off in a slow parade. He guessed they wouldn't go far.

That was confirmed when Constable Boulanger walked up to them. His face was shadowed by the broad brim of his hat, but Lucas could tell he was scowling when the Royal Canadian Mounted Police officer scolded, "You shouldn't come out here to the main road together. It causes a feeding frenzy."

"We needed to talk to you, Constable," Lucas said.

The officer stepped closer. "About what?" He pulled out a notebook and began taking notes as Lucas—with help from Aveline—explained what they'd discussed about Julie's kidnapping.

"We hope we're wrong," Aveline said when Lucas had finished.

Constable Boulanger glanced down at his notes and sighed. "I don't think you are."

"Have you talked to Mr. DeSare about it?"

"My superiors have."

Lucas heard Aveline's sigh of relief and felt a weight as heavy as the road lift off his shoulders.

Should they mention the other problem bothering them? The question of the propped-open gate and the damaged harvester being related.

He looked at Aveline, and she gave the faintest shake of her head. She didn't want him telling the constable. He had to agree, because the connection seemed tenuous.

Yet, if they were wrong and there *was* a connection…

No, he wasn't going to think of that. The important thing was making sure a girl wasn't put in danger again.

Aveline wiggled her left fingers as she carried a basket of green beans into the empty kitchen. The simple motion hurt her arm, but not as much as it had yesterday. The wound was healing, and soon she'd be allowed to spend time working on the cheese. *Daed* had insisted she stay away until her stitches were out.

"We can't see germs with our eyes," he'd said.

"The *doktor* assured me there are no signs of infection. I wouldn't pass along anything to the cheese."

Daed had given her one of his kind smiles that crinkled his eyes. "I'm not worried about you causing a problem for the cheese. I'm worried about the cheese-making process causing *you* a problem."

That was *Daed*. Always keeping his family foremost in his thoughts. In that way, her parents were much same. The big difference was in how they showed their concern. *Daed* wanted them to have a roof over their heads and enough to eat. *Mamm* was focused on finding them each a spouse so they could have their own homes and families.

It also meant Aveline's day must be spent in the house doing chores instead of working with the animals or overseeing the process of making cheese. With the calves weaned, there was plenty of water buffalo milk for cheese. She loved adding the bright green-and-white labels that read *Lampel Red Earth Mozzarella Cheese. Made in Prince Edward Island.*

Tipping the basket into the sink, Aveline began washing dirt off the beans. She picked out dried leaves that had come off along with the beans. She tossed them in the wastebasket as she continued to rinse the vegetables, taking care not to rub off their fine nap. Scooping them up, she dropped them into a bowl she'd put on the counter before she'd gone out to the garden.

She got out her favorite small knife and a cutting board. It was quick work to take off both ends of the beans and cut them into smaller pieces. She intended to make chow-chow. Her family used a recipe that included green beans, and she looked forward to the crisp crunch.

As her knife thudded against the wooden board, she couldn't silence the thoughts that had plagued her in the garden. Should she and Lucas have told Constable Boulanger yesterday about the incidents on their farms? She'd worried if they'd dumped another flurry of concerns on him, he couldn't focus on protecting Julie.

Yet, Moobeam needed to be kept safe, too. Aveline hadn't said anything to *Daed*, either, just closed the gate. She'd carried the stones to the pond where the water buffalo loved to submerge themselves on a hot, sunny day. She'd dropped them in, trusting the deep *thunks* concluded what she hoped was a prank someone was playing on her brothers. Maybe she should mention to them that—

She pushed aside her thoughts when *Mamm* came in with a handful of bright pink coneflowers. Walking to the sink, she opened the cupboard underneath and pulled out a clear vase. She put the flowers in them and added water before carrying them to the table. Putting them in the center, she appraised them and smiled.

Not at the flowers, Aveline discovered when *Mamm* said, "I heard you and Lucas were surrounded by reporters yesterday."

"*Ja*."

"You didn't mention it."

"There was nothing to mention. I was retrieving Moobeam, and the constable sent the reporters away."

"That calf!" *Mamm* spat. "She doesn't have a bit of sense."

"She's a *boppli*."

"A big one."

Aveline knew when to quit a conversation she'd never win. As she finished chopping green beans, she asked, "Do you think *Daed* would like a batch of chow-chow with hot peppers in it? I saw some are ready to be picked."

Mamm wouldn't be sidetracked. "I understand why Rodney didn't want you talking to the press, but it's a shame you can't."

"What do you mean?" She wiped down the counter, taking care not to brush her sore arm against it.

"Who knows who might have seen the article? Men are impressed by a brave *maedel*."

Aveline didn't have to hear the slight emphasis *Mamm* put on the word *maedel*. Scrubbing a stubborn glob of flour she'd missed after baking that morning, she said, "It doesn't matter, *Mamm*. Rodney has been clear he doesn't want Lucas and me talking to them."

"Lucas *and* you? You were at his farm yesterday when the reporters found you. Is there something you are keeping secret?"

"*Mamm*, there's nothing. If Moobeam didn't keep wandering over there to see his goats, I wouldn't have a single reason to talk to him." Knowing that wasn't the truth, she felt compelled to add, "Moobeam and our worry about something else happening to Julie DeSare."

She wished she'd remained quiet when she heard *Daed* say behind her, "You shouldn't fret about that. Just because God used you and Lucas as His tool to save the *Englisch* girl is no reason for you to fret about it."

Aveline looked from one parent to the other. They were in complete agreement. Arguing with them would be as fruitless as debating *Mamm* about the importance of finding a spouse.

She knew that, but the words pushed past her lips. "We've got a *gut* reason to worry. The man in jail may not be the one who planned the crime."

"You know this how?" *Daed*'s voice was inflexible as he sat at the table and gestured her to do the same. "You can't let your imagination run away with you."

Aveline explained what she and Lucas had discussed.

"Did you mention this to the police?" *Daed* asked as soon as she was done.

"*Ja.*"

"Then you've done all you can." He reached across the table and patted her clenched hands. "Aveline, God put you in the right place at the right time. Now He has put the police in the right place." Not giving her a chance to respond, he went on. "I'm meeting with Rodney after church this coming Sunday to discuss the reward money."

"And with Lucas?"

He shook his head. "Rodney asked Juan to join us."

"Why's he asking Lucas's brother instead?"

"Because the money wasn't offered to Juan as it wasn't offered to me. He thinks this would be better."

Though she didn't agree, she nodded. She'd hoped her share of the money could go to the Mennonite Disaster Service, which helped anyone—plain or not—in the wake of disaster.

"I don't want the *Englisch* girl and her abduction discussed in our home any longer, Aveline," *Daed* said when she didn't answer. "Do you understand?"

She did understand he was hoping to prevent her from worrying, so she nodded. What he didn't understand was how fearful she was that they were at the beginning of trouble, not the end.

Chapter Six

The knock on the front door came as Aveline was walking down the stairs with a basket of laundry. The constables had been successful at keeping the reporters away from the house, but maybe one had thrown caution to the wind in their determination to be the first to publish an interview with her or Lucas.

If we sat with them, maybe they'd leave us alone.

She scowled at the thought. Talking to one wouldn't put an end to it. The others would want their chance to tell the story. She was thankful the RCMP officers were keeping the reporters away.

Her hand tightened on the basket. Had Constable Boulanger gone to his superiors and asked them to plead with Mr. DeSare to be cautious and make sure his daughter was protected? She recalled the resolve in Julie's *daed*'s eyes when he'd come to the house. Nothing and no one would have a chance to endanger his daughter if he could help it. Would that be enough?

Many questions and no answers. Her family refused to talk about what had happened. Only one person seemed as unsettled by the events as she was.

Lucas.

Yet, talking to him added to her worries, not lessened them. Though she shouldn't care, she was bothered that he'd flirted with every woman except her. Not that she wanted him to tease her and try to make her giggle and lean in on him as she'd seen other women do. It irked her that he seemed as attracted to her as he would have been to Moobeam.

She could be reading him wrong. He could be refraining from flirting with her because he wished she'd leave him alone. Was it because she'd flirted with his cousin in a desperate, wasted attempt to satisfy *Mamm*? His whole family had kept her at arm's length since then.

If that were so, why had Lucas motioned for her to follow him into his equipment shed and asked what was bothering her? None of it made any sense.

Knuckles rapped harder against the door, yanking Aveline back to the present. Balancing the basket on her hip, she looked around. Nobody else was in the house. She sighed. If she didn't answer the door, the reporter—assuming it was a member of the press on the porch—might head around the house and find her *mamm* in the garden. Aveline didn't want *Mamm* talking to reporters because *Mamm* might still harbor the idea of getting her daughter mentioned in the newspaper like a lonely hearts column reject.

Rushing down the last few steps, she set the basket on the couch. She opened the door to find a tall, dark-haired man wearing a severe black suit with an unadorned black tie and a neatly pressed white shirt on the other side.

"I'm not a reporter," he said before she could speak.

"I'd like to believe you—"

The man in a black suit held out an envelope to her. She noticed he had a flat, black cap in his other hand. "Mr. DeSare asked me to deliver this to you. If you would be so kind as to open it and read it, I can take your response to him."

"Mr. DeSare?" She sounded like a parrot echoing the man's words, but she hadn't expected to hear from Julie's *daed* until after he and the bishop had met for a discussion about the reward. Had the meeting already happened? Impossible because the bishop wasn't meeting with *Daed* until Sunday. Any meeting with Mr. DeSare would come after that.

"Will you read it?" He gestured with the envelope.

"*Ja.*"

Taking the envelope, she saw it wasn't sealed. Mr. DeSare must trust this man not to read the message.

Or, the rational portion of her brain argued, *it's such an innocuous note he doesn't care if someone reads it before you do.*

She opened the envelope and drew out a single piece of paper. It was thick and embossed with Mr. DeSare's name in a fancy, gilded script on top. However, the handwritten letter was simple and to the point.

Aveline, I trust this finds you well. I'm writing to let you know Julie would like to see you and Lucas. Would you please come to our house for a visit tomorrow at 1:00 p.m.? I'll send a car for you. Please let Randall know if it's possible for you to visit. Julie would be grateful, and so would I.

It was signed with Philip DeSare's name written in a grand flourish that matched the printed version at the top of the page.

Too many different emotions to count burst through her. Pleasure that Julie wanted to see them. That was mixed with anxiety. Had Mr.

DeSare written because his daughter was in deep distress over what had happened to her? Both were joined by the relief that she'd be able to see how well the girl was doing. Hope entwined through everything. Hope she'd be able to judge if Julie's *daed* comprehended the danger his daughter might be in.

It added up to one possible answer to the invitation.

"Are you Randall?" Aveline asked the man on the porch.

"I am. Do you have a response for Mr. DeSare?"

"*Ja.* Tell him I'll be happy to visit tomorrow. I'll pass along the message to Lucas, and I'm sure he'll want to join us if he can."

"Thank you, Miss Lampel." He put on his cap. "I'll let Mr. DeSare know. I'll be back around noon tomorrow." He tipped his cap before walking to a large black car she hadn't noticed in her shock of discovering the *Englischer* on the other side of the door.

Closing it, Aveline wasn't surprised to see *Mamm* standing on the other side of the room in the kitchen doorway.

"Who was that?" *Mamm* asked with suspicious eyes. As much as *Mamm* wanted Aveline married, she wouldn't be happy if Aveline fell in love with an *Englischer*.

"A man who works for Mr. DeSare."

"You know your *daed* doesn't want you having anything to do with that family and that situation."

She did know, and guilt taunted her. Going against her *daed*'s direct order wasn't something she should do. She wished she could have had a chance to speak with *Daed* before she'd had to give Randall—was it Mr. Randall or was that his given name?—an answer.

Because she couldn't defend herself against *Mamm*'s accusation, she said, "Julie—the girl we found—is inviting Lucas and me to their house tomorrow afternoon."

"You and Lucas?" *Mamm*'s whole demeanor shifted. "How nice! You can enjoy a pleasant drive to the shore, have a visit with that poor, frightened girl, and then a pleasant ride home. You and Lucas will have plenty of time together. It must be at least two hours to drive there."

"Two-and-a-half hours by buggy, which is why Mr. DeSare is sending his car."

Mamm smiled. "Even better. Lucas won't have to worry about driving unfamiliar roads. You two can take time during the ride to get to know each other better." Her smile faded. "Don't get moony over what you'll see in that big house. We may not have those fancy gizmos, but we've got what we need to live the life God has given us."

"I know that, *Mamm*, but I need to let Lucas know about the invitation."

Mamm's smile fell away. "I thought you said Mr. DeSare invited him, too."

"The invitation came here, and I said I'd let Lucas know."

Aveline answered a few more questions she found irrelevant before she slipped out while *Mamm* was beginning to list items that could go in a basket she wanted to send to Julie. Breathing a big sigh of relief, Aveline rushed down the farm lane. She turned away from the road and clung to the shadows of the trees edging it. Whenever a car approached, she slid behind a tree or a bush so she couldn't be seen.

How much longer would this go on? She'd been sure the reporters would find another story to chase by now. A chill slithered down her spine. Would her visit to the DeSare house rekindle the media's curiosity about her and Lucas?

"I don't need that," she muttered as she passed the Overgard farm and headed toward Lucas's brother's place. "*Mamm* already is curious enough for everyone in the world."

Releasing her breath as she reached Lucas's lane, she was astonished at how long she'd been holding it as she crept along the road. She took another deep breath and relaxed as she walked toward Lucas's barn. It was a lovely summer day and she shouldn't be sullying it with worry. The muddy scent of the river mixed with the heat rising off the red sand fields. Rows of potato hills marched into the distance. Soon that precision would be replaced by clods of dirt after the hills had been opened and the potatoes removed.

Aveline wasn't surprised to find Lucas working on his harvester. Most of the digging arms were now straight. He was so focused on his work, he must not have noticed her approach because he started when she spoke his name.

Jumping to his feet, he scowled. "I told you—" His eyes widened. "Oh, Aveline, I'm sorry. I didn't know it was you. A couple of those idiotic reporters slipped onto the farm about an hour ago."

"Did they leave when you reminded them they weren't supposed to be on private property?"

He rolled his eyes as a weary grin lightened his features. "They seemed to believe my lane is a public throughway."

"Something that would have been *gut* for you to know last winter when you had to plow it yourself."

"*Ja.*" He chuckled. "I didn't argue with them. I left that to the cops. You may not be surprised the reporters decided they didn't want to argue any more when a police car rolled in here."

Aveline hesitated before saying, "I agreed to something that may cause us trouble."

"What?"

She explained the invitation she'd received. "I didn't think until I was on the way over here about how going to the DeSares' might catch the media's attention."

Resting against the half wall as he had during their previous conversation there, he said, "I don't like you thinking that way, Aveline."

"What do you mean?"

"You shouldn't have to feel paranoid."

"You don't?"

He laughed. "I've got proof someone is after me."

Knowing he was trying to help, she struggled to smile. She failed. "Mr. DeSare will be sending the car to my house around noon tomorrow."

"I can't go."

She should have been suffused with relief at his answer, because traveling to the DeSare house on her own would countermand her *mamm*'s anticipation of what might happen while Aveline was with Lucas. *Stop being silly*, she chided. Truth be told, she would have appreciated Lucas's company when she was driven across the Island to the other shore.

"That's too bad," Aveline said, knowing she

couldn't let the silence linger. "Julie wants to see both of us."

"I know, but I can't get away tomorrow." He pointed to a bucket that held potatoes. "I dug those by hand a while ago. They're about ready. I've got to focus on the harvest from this point forward."

"Julie will be disappointed."

"So will I. I would have liked to see for myself that she's doing okay. Do you think Mr. DeSare has another reason for asking us there?"

"No. His note was a simple invitation. Time and place." She paused then said, "He mentioned Julie would be grateful for our visit. I suspect she's feeling cooped up in their house."

"Why do you say that?"

"If my *kind* was kidnapped, I don't think I'd let him or her out of my sight."

He looked at the pail by his feet. "I see what you mean."

"I'm hoping my visit will help ease Julie's loneliness." Knowing how torn he must be between taking care of his crop and helping the girl, she added, "I can let you know how it goes, if you'd like."

Relief eased the lines in his forehead. "I would. You'll have to—" His brows lowered as he looked past her toward the road.

"What's wrong?"

"I thought I saw a truck slowing down, but it looks like they were turning up the road."

"Guess who's paranoid now?" She started to laugh, then realized he wasn't. She didn't like how they'd been changed by the events surrounding Julie's kidnapping, but had no idea how either of them could revert back to the people they'd been.

Lucas frowned again. Not at Aveline. He wasn't upset with her. No, maybe he was, because he was unsettled by everything and everyone right now. "I've got *gut* reason to be paranoid." Tapping the bucket with his toe, he added, "If one of them gets into his or her head to go through the fields, it could ruin part of the harvest."

"They're not going to do that. They're Islanders. They know the importance of the harvest."

"I'm not sure what they know."

Aveline put her hand out toward him before drawing it back. "I assumed something else would have grabbed their attention by now."

He was adding to her distress. That hadn't been his intention, but her fingers shook. He wouldn't be dishonest. She needed to be on the alert to avoid the media.

"Prince Edward Island," he said with the best smile he could manage, "isn't a hotbed of news, so the abduction of Philip DeSare's *kind* isn't a story that's going anywhere soon."

She ran her fingers over the top of the harvester. "I wish we could give them another story to take their attention off us."

"What did you have in mind? A plague of locusts maybe?" His grin now felt more natural. "I think we've got those already. We just call them mosquitoes."

"Calling those reporters locusts isn't nice."

"I wasn't referring to the reporters, but are you calling them a plague?"

She smiled. "Don't twist my words. I don't need to have to watch everything I say around you, too."

"You're right. I'm sorry. You've got to admit the press is about as welcome as a mosquito swarm."

Laughing, she said, "True. So what are we going to do?"

Instead of laughing, he replied, "I don't know. It's clear they aren't giving up."

"*Daed* is going to speak with Rodney about the reward after church on Sunday."

He stood straighter, wondering why the bishop hadn't let him know. "I should be there."

"He suggested Juan be there instead."

"Why?" He couldn't imagine any reason to send his brother to the meeting in his place.

"*Daed* didn't answer when I asked him that question. I suspect they think we might not make the best choices after holding the checks in our hands."

A pulse of anger swelled through him and his voice grew hard. "Why would they think that? We've already declined taking the reward. We did that right in front of your family."

"*Daed* says—"

"Does Elam think we've changed our minds?" He narrowed his eyes as she looked away. "Have *you* changed your mind?"

She turned to face him and he saw her distress. At the situation or at his question?

"No," she said without a hint of the emotion flaring in her eyes. "Why would you think that?"

"Fixing the fences so Moobeam and the other water buffalo don't escape can't be cheap. There's the damage to the gate and—"

"We'll pay for the repairs, just like we do with everything else on the farm. With the money we've made from selling our cheese." She walked out of the shed so fast, he had to half run to catch up with her.

He called her name, but she kept on walking. Reaching out, he caught her arm to stop her. When she gave a soft mew of pain, he yanked his hand away from her left arm. She cradled her arm as she stopped.

Lucas thought of a dozen different things to say to her but what came out was, "Aveline, I'm sorry."

When she faced him, he saw her confusion. She wasn't sure what he was apologizing for. For hurting her by mistake? For yelling at her in the shed? For having to focus on his potatoes instead of going with her to see Julie DeSare? For taking his frustration out on her?

"It's okay, Lucas." Her voice was so soft it could have been the breeze off the river.

She was accepting his apology, though she didn't know why he was asking her forgiveness. How could that be? Whispers spoke of her being self-centered and arrogant and resolved to let nobody get in her way. That described Chalonna Lampel. Had the faults of the *mamm* been attached to the daughter, even if she didn't deserve it?

"It's okay," Aveline repeated, and he realized she'd interpreted his silence as disbelief.

That wasn't far off from the truth. He couldn't believe he continued to let rumors about her outweigh what he'd seen with his own eyes.

"I would have liked to see Julie tomorrow," he said because it was the simplest thing and the truth.

"I'll let her know that."

He wanted to make things right, but he couldn't

blurt out that he was baffled by how different she was from the tales shared on the Amish grapevine. Then he'd have to explain how he couldn't get the gossip out of his head.

You'd have to explain how you can't get her out of your head.

He ignored the flicker of truth coming to life in his brain. He needed to focus on his harvest instead of Aveline. He ignored the image of her *mamm*'s self-satisfied smile if she discovered he was making an effort to know her daughter better.

"I could try to distract the reporters," Lucas said.

"You would?" Her lips parted with her surprise, and he had to force himself to look away and stop wondering how they might taste. "I appreciate the offer, but it's not necessary. No reporters came to the house while Randall was delivering the invitation. He may be able to slip in again without them seeing him."

"The offer stands, though I'm glad it may not be necessary."

She stood straight, releasing her injured arm. Tilting her head as if she were a bird, she said, "If anyone had asked me about you talking to reporters before this began, I would have said you'd be glad to."

"You would have?"

"You always are one of the first to talk to new-comers among us. You seem to know the right thing to say. I'm so nervous, I stumble over every other word I speak."

"You couldn't have been listening closely because I stumble over *every* word when I'm nervous."

She relaxed. "*Danki*. I know you're joking but—"

"I'm not."

Her bright green eyes grew as round as her mouth before she asked, "You're not?"

He shook his head. "I'm not. I've been trying to avoid the *Englisch* reporters. You and I know this may not be over. Mr. DeSare does as well. You could see it when he was at your house."

"I guessed it was because he was worried about any lingering effects the kidnapping might have on Julie."

"There's that, but he was as anxious as a cat in a kennel."

"And, for him, it wasn't *Mamm* making him nervous."

He opened his mouth then shut it as he saw a twinkle in her eyes. "Are you suggesting that *I* was nervous because of your *mamm*?"

"*Ja.*" She rubbed her palms together. "I can't pretend to be oblivious to my *mamm*'s match-making ways. If someone looks my way for ten seconds, she's eager to call the deacon. You were patient with her when you brought Moobeam back."

"Really?" He hadn't thought he was patient. He'd been looking for every possible excuse to leave.

"I've seen a woman cut and run when *Mamm* gave her what Wes calls her 'gotcha now' look. My brothers knew they had to find strong women to deal with *Mamm*'s powerful personality."

"From what I've heard, they have."

"*Ja*. For the first time in years, the celery *Mamm* insisted *Daed* clear extra garden rows for will be used the way she's been praying it would." She kneaded her hands together, and he realized how talking about Chalonna and her matchmaking ways made her nervous. "Of course, with my brothers set, it's my turn."

"You don't need to worry."

"What do you mean?" Her voice took on a whetted edge.

Realizing that his words could have been taken as an insult, he hurried to say, "Everyone around here is well acquainted with Chalonna and her ways. Nobody is going to think badly of you because of them."

"No. They're going to feel sorry for me." Raising her chin, she added, "I'll let you know how the visit goes and how Julie is doing."

He didn't have a chance to answer as Aveline walked away, looking tinier against the empty road. They'd talked about how alone and trapped Julie must have been feeling. Nobody had mentioned how Aveline might feel the same. Chalonna's efforts to marry off her *kinder* isolated her daughter in ways Lucas had failed to notice.

He wouldn't make that heartless assumption again.

Chapter Seven

Aveline stepped out of the black car and into a world she'd never imagined. The massive stucco house beyond a fountain blocked her view of the dunes and the ocean. Cedar shingles that were beginning to turn gray from the salt air covered the house from the third-story's widow's walk to the wild grasses that edged the decks sprouting in every direction. When Randall, who'd driven her across the narrow finger of Prince Edward Island motioned for her to follow, she did, but paused by the fountain. In the center was a round, flat stone that looked like it should be a glossy-topped table. Water washed over the surface and dropped into a concrete base large enough for Moobeam to wallow in.

"Do you like it?" asked a young voice.

She smiled as Julie stepped off the deck at the edge of the driveway. Unlike the last time she'd seen the girl, Julie's hair was brushed and her face clean. She wore a red blouse under a denim vest that was several shades darker than her shorts. Big artificial flowers decorated her pink flip-flops. Remnants of healing scratches on her legs and lower arms were the only outward signs of her ordeal.

"I think," Aveline answered, "your house is lovely, but not as lovely as seeing you."

When she held out her arms, Julie ran to fling her own around Aveline. Having the stitches out yesterday had released the tension along Aveline's left arm and she could hold the girl close with barely a hint of pain. They hugged for a moment before Julie pulled back and asked, "Where's Lucas?"

"He couldn't join us today. He'll *komm* another time, I'm sure," she added, though she shouldn't commit Lucas to a visit.

Julie glanced at Randall. "Thank you for bringing Aveline here. I'll let you know when she's ready to leave."

"You're welcome, Miss Julie. The car will be ready when Miss Lampel is." He tipped his cap, then walked around the side of the house toward a garage that was as big as the Lampels' rambling farmhouse.

"Do you want to look around?" Julie asked.

"I came to see you, not the house."

The *kind* didn't giggle as Aveline had hoped. "Daddy said I should show you around. That's what he does whenever we have someone visit for the first time."

"Then show me around." She gestured at the fountain. "Why do you have this in the middle of your driveway? Do you have a horse or two you need to make sure have a drink? Maybe my *daed* should get something like this."

Julie shook her head. "No, no horses, though I've been telling Daddy we need some so we can ride on the beach like they do on TV. You don't watch TV, do you?"

"We don't have one, but I've seen them in stores and restaurants."

"Oh." The girl began to chatter like one of the gulls soaring on the salty breeze, but something was amiss to Aveline's ear. The *kind* spoke as if by rote. "We use geothermal heat. The process gives off a lot of water, and it needs to go somewhere. Daddy decided to have a fountain and let it drain away into a pond. That way, it doesn't hurt the house's foundation or the dunes."

"You know a lot about this."

Julie gave a casual shrug. "Not as much as Daddy. If you want to know more, ask him, but he'll talk and talk until your brain explodes." She motioned for Aveline to follow her to the front door. "Come in. Maurie has lemonade and cookies ready for us."

"Maurie?"

"Her real name is Maureen Francis. She's our cook."

Aveline had intended to ask another question, but every word she knew vanished from her head when she entered the house. The ceiling rose almost seven meters from the slate floor. She hadn't expected to see cedar shakes on the wall in front of her. Landscapes in soft colors hung on the wall between lobster trap buoys.

When she managed to get her feet to move, she went around the wall with the girl. This time, she couldn't hold back her gasp as she stared at a huge stone hearth. The stones were various shades of red, and she knew they'd come from somewhere on the Island. Across from the fireplace and beyond a huge fan that had claimed the apex of the vaulted ceiling, was a triangular collection of windows that climbed as high as the stone wall. The view of the ocean brought a prayer of gratitude to her lips. How blessed she was to be able to see this glorious vista made by His *wunderbaar* hands! She wished Lucas could share it.

Lucas? *Get out of my head!* If *Mamm* knew Aveline had him on her mind, *Mamm* would redouble her matchmaking efforts.

Her delight in being with Julie faltered. She hadn't told *Mamm* Lucas wasn't coming to the DeSares', worried Aveline would be forbidden to go alone.

A woman in a black dress and a white apron came into the room, carrying a tray. She set it on a table near a bright blue sofa.

"Thank you, Sandra," Julie said, motioning for Aveline to join her by the couch.

Aveline gave the woman in the black dress a smile and added her thanks before sitting next to Julie. Lowering her voice, she said, "I thought her name is Maurie."

"No. Maurie is our cook. Sandra is a maid."

"I see." She reached for a cookie that looked as if it might be lemon-flavored.

A house with one person to cook and another to serve? And another whose job seemed to be driving the car? Mr. DeSare must be wealthier than she'd guessed.

She pushed aside her thoughts and began to talk with the *kind* who had questions about Moobeam and Lucas as well as Aveline's family.

"Two brothers?" Julie asked. "I've always wanted a brother or sister." She selected a brown-and-pink cookie. "I have a half sister and two half brothers, but I never see them."

"Why not?"

"Because they live with Antonio in Vancouver. Antonio was Mommy's first husband."

Though she had known *Englischers* could end their marriages, among the Amish, it was assumed marriage was for life. A plain widow or widower could remarry, but any *kinder* were merged together, not separated by a continent.

Julie didn't seem to notice her silence. Instead, she offered Aveline another cookie. When Aveline took what looked like an oatmeal cookie, the girl asked in a near whisper, "Can I tell you something?"

"Anything."

"Someone's been watching our house."

Aveline stiffened. She'd expected Julie to confide a childish whim. Not to speak of such a serious matter. Picking her words with care, because she didn't want Julie to think she was dismissing the girl's worry, she asked, "What makes you think that?"

"I see shadows out by the dunes."

"They could be people enjoying the beach."

"I thought about that, but I don't see that many people there during the day. Only at night."

An idea struck Aveline. "Could your *daed* have hired security?"

"Oh, I didn't think of that." She stood and hugged herself. "He tells me not to worry, but he is."

"That's his responsibility. He's your *daed*. Parents always worry about their *kinder*."

"Do yours?"

"You've got no idea how much they worry!" Nobody worried more than her *mamm* about getting her sons and daughter married.

Her answer seemed to calm the girl. Dropping to sit on the sofa, she said, "You don't think I'm making this up, do you?"

"No, of course not," she hurried to say as she realized how little she knew about the *kind*. Could what Julie had endured when she was abducted have made her imagination go wild? Asking the girl wouldn't help when she needed to be believed.

"Miss Julie?" came a voice from near the entry. "Miss Julie, you've got another caller."

The *kind* jumped up, Dismay erased from her face as she ran, her flip-flops slapping the stone floor.

Aveline looked over her shoulder, and her gasp escaped as her gaze was caught by Lucas's. He was dressed in a neatly pressed light blue shirt. His black suspenders were clipped to black trousers that appeared new. His shoes had been buffed to a hint of a shine.

"Lucas!" Julie cried. "I thought you couldn't get away today." She gave him an enthusiastic embrace.

The tips of his ears turned red, which Aveline

found charming as he continued toward where she sat. Julie walked beside him.

"I realized," he said, "taking one afternoon to visit you, Julie, was worth letting the potatoes sit in the ground for a little longer." He gave her a grin that would have better suited a naughty boy.

Aveline bit her trembling lower lip. There *was* more to Lucas than people claimed. She poured him a glass of lemonade so she could compose her face, while Julie filled him in on the conversation.

"Just at night," Julie was saying as she sat between Aveline and Lucas. "Who do you think is out there, Lucas?"

Intruding into their conversation before Julie's fears overwhelmed her, Aveline said, "I mentioned that Julie should check with her *daed* and see if he knows. He might have someone keeping an eye on the house and you." She tapped Julie on the nose. "You'd better keep this clean, young lady."

She didn't get the giggle she'd hoped for. Over the *kind*'s head, Lucas shot her a curious glance.

Not now, she mouthed.

He nodded, but she couldn't miss the curiosity emblazoned on his face. It vanished the second before Julie looked at him.

The time passed quickly. Julie insisted they visit her room. A cacophony of pink as gaudy as her flip-flops, it had pale curtains that looked like spun cotton candy. The furniture was white with gold accents and glass knobs with flowers inside them. Toys and books were placed on shelves, and not a hint of dust was visible on them or on the desk with its computer or on the pink-and-green rug under their feet. Aveline assumed the two sets of slatted doors led to closets, but Julie opened one to reveal a bathroom as pink as her room. If she hadn't known before, it was obvious Mr. DeSare doted on his daughter.

When they returned to the living room after being introduced to Julie's favorite teddy bear named Cuddles, two men walked into the room from the opposite direction.

"I'll review the report, Neal," Mr. DeSare said to the other *Englischer*.

That man wasn't as tall as Julie's *daed*, and his long face was narrow. His thinning hair was a combination of blond and gray. His suit was the same dull color as those streaks. A white shirt and sedate blue tie seemed out of place in the beach house because Mr. DeSare was wearing an open-necked bright green knit shirt and khakis. His feet were bare.

"Right away, I hope," the man Mr. DeSare had called Neal replied. "It's got information I hadn't anticipated. If we jump on it, we can minimize any repercussions."

Mr. DeSare started to answer, then realized the two men weren't alone. A smile spread his face. "I'd hoped I'd get a chance to see you this afternoon." He strode forward and shook Lucas's hand, nodding at Aveline before tucking his daughter under his arm for a hug. Motioning with his other hand to his companion, he said, "C'mon over here, Neal. I want you to meet some pretty special people. Neal Mathers, this is Aveline Lampel and Lucas Kuepfer. They're—"

"You're the folks who found Julie." He smiled as he offered his hand to Lucas and then to her. "You'll never know how grateful Philip is to you two for bringing his precious daughter home safe and sound."

"*Danki*—I mean, thank you," Aveline murmured. "I'm grateful God put us in a place where we could be of help."

"I agree." Mr. DeSare glanced at the other man. "How about we continue the discussion at the four o'clock meeting, Neal?"

Nodding, Neal walked away without another word. When he glanced back, Aveline saw his frustrated frown. However, she was glad Mr. DeSare was putting his daughter ahead of business. Then she wondered if she'd misread their host's intentions because, after talking with his daughter for a few minutes, he asked her to leave the three of them.

"To talk about grown-up stuff?" Julie asked.

"Yes." He winked but faltered when she didn't react. "Boring adult stuff."

"Don't leave without coming to see me. Okay?"

The girl was so somber, Aveline took the *kind*'s hands as she said, "You have our word."

"Okay." The answer was so reluctant and disbelieving, Aveline squeezed her hands.

Mr. DeSare waited for his daughter to move out of earshot before saying, "She used to be trusting. Now she finds it difficult to trust anyone, even me."

"That's understandable," Lucas said.

"I hate seeing her so fearful."

Aveline didn't hesitate. "Mr. DeSare, Julie told us she's seeing shadowed figures at night. Out on the beach. I told her you might have hired someone to watch over the house and over her. It was just a guess, but I wanted her to be less fearful."

"A good guess, Aveline," he said as he selected a chair facing the sofa and motioned for them to sit. "I've hired a security company. I didn't want to scare Julie, so I didn't tell her."

"Sometimes what we don't know frightens us more than what we do know," Lucas said as he sat on the couch a cushion away from Aveline.

"I hadn't considered that. All I can think of is making sure nothing bad will happen to her." He tapped one finger against his chin. "Oh, I know bad things happen, but I want them to be *normal* bad things like a boy breaking her heart or her failing a test she thought she'd pass. Not like this incident."

"I understand what you mean." She wondered why he'd chosen "incident" to describe his daughter's kidnapping. Maybe he couldn't say the word *kidnapping*. Knowing she needed to add more, she said, "Julie seems lonely."

"She is. That's why I asked you to visit. I hope you'll come whenever you can. I wish I knew other ways to help her, but I don't. Not when I can't bear to let her out of my sight. If something else was to happen to her…"

Her heart filled with renewed grief when he lowered his face into his hands. How could she and Lucas complain about how the girl's abduction had changed their lives when Julie and Mr. DeSare were devastated? Dealing with nosy reporters was nothing compared to fearing a loved one would be hurt, or worse.

"We pray for both of you," Lucas said.

When the other man raised his head, she realized Lucas had again found the perfect thing to say. She couldn't help admiring and envying that skill.

"Thank you," Mr. DeSare whispered. "I appreciate that."

"You don't need to thank us. We're blessed to

have met your daughter. I know Aveline wishes, as I do, it'd been under different circumstances, Mr. DeSare."

"Call me Philip. We've gone through enough with this incident to be considered family at this point." He sighed. "Family is what she needs. I'm an only child, too, so I know how tough it can be. At least, I lived where there were other children to play with. When I bought this place, there were plans for more houses to be built nearby, and I was sure she'd have plenty of playmates. Neither the houses nor the playmates have materialized so far."

Aveline sat straighter. "If you'd like, I can introduce her to the kids in our district. They'll welcome her to play with them. Of course, if she spends time with us, she'll have chores to do as the others do, if that's okay with you."

"Chores are fine. I had them when I was a kid, and she has some." He rested his elbows on his chair arms and clasped his hands between his knees. "The simple truth is, since the incident, I don't like her to be where I can't keep an eye on her."

"I'll watch her closely." She paused, realizing how difficult it had been for him to admit his fear. "If you're willing to trust us with her."

"Can I get back to you on your generous offer?" He glanced at the heavy gold watch on his wrist. "I'll have to ask you to excuse me. I've got a phone call I can't delay. Would it be okay if I let you know in a couple of days?"

"Take all the time you need," Lucas said.

She glanced at him. Was he saying he wanted to help her help the girl? It would mean lots of interaction with him. She waited for dismay to rush into her gut. Instead, a sense of anticipation rose through her as she thought of spending time with him as they worked to make the girl laugh.

Something more had changed and she wasn't sure it was for the better. Not that it mattered. She needed to do what she could to make Julie smile.

Lucas held the door while Aveline got out in front of her house. Closing it, he waved to the driver and watched as the large car maneuvered several times until it drove out toward the main road. He glanced at the house but didn't see anyone peering out the windows.

Gut! That meant Chalonna wasn't about to pounce on him. It wouldn't take her long to figure out the sound of the car meant her daughter was home. He'd better get off the Lampels' farm fast.

Did Aveline know that? Of course she did, because she said, "*Danki* for joining me at the De-Sares' house, Lucas. It meant a lot to Julie. Did you see how her eyes lit when you came into the room?"

He almost said he hadn't noticed because he'd been looking at Aveline, her hair awash in the sunlight reflecting off the ocean. "I could tell she was happy to see us."

"So was Philip, though he's on edge. His face and the rest of him don't always show the same reaction to what others say. Or maybe it's a response to what he's thinking." He must have looked baffled, because she hurried on to say, "I'll give you an example. When the other man—"

"Neal?" he suggested.

"*Ja.* Neal. When he was in the room with us, Mr. De—Philip was smiling, but there was a tension between the men that was so strong it was almost visible."

He raised his hands and shrugged. "You've lost me."

"Okay. I'll make it simple. Neal was smiling, but he was standing on the balls of his feet as if he were preparing to rush somewhere."

"They're busy men."

She nodded. "They are, but watch Neal if you see him again. You may get what I mean."

"*Englischers*—"

"This isn't an *Englisch* or a plain thing. It's a human thing. We give ourselves away at one time or another."

"So tell me what I'm thinking now."

Shaking her head, she smiled. "It doesn't work like that, Lucas. Nobody's reading anyone's mind. It's about how we're feeling."

Why had he continued this conversation? He wanted to leave to avoid Chalonna, and his animals were waiting for supper, and he needed to make his own meal and put away the clothes Annalise had laundered for him yesterday…or had it been the day before?

"You're eager to get out of here," Aveline said, drawing his attention to her. "Just like Neal, you're balancing yourself on your toes. You want to head home because you're upset."

"I'm not upset."

"You *are* upset. Otherwise, why would you be standing with your arms crossed across your chest? You're cutting yourself off from the world, keeping everyone out so they can't guess how you're feeling." She arched her brows. "See that? It's my way of telling you without words you should be awed by what I said."

He started to give her a teasing reply, then heard the screen door on the porch open. Saying a swift good-bye, he hurried toward the road. At the moment, the thought of running into the reporters was preferable to facing her matchmaking *mamm*.

Chapter Eight

"Don't plan anything for a week from Saturday," *Mamm* said as Aveline came into the kitchen three days later carrying a basket filled with the peas she'd been picking in the garden. "I told Mattie Kuhns we'd be there to help with the *redding* up before they host the next church service."

Aveline smiled as she put the basket on the table. "That sounds like fun."

The wrong answer because *Mamm* frowned. "Aveline, you think about the wrong kinds of fun. Instead of washing down walls and mopping floors, you should be looking forward to going to youth game nights and singing."

"Those youth events are for younger people."

"They are for *unmarried* people. Until you're married, you should attend."

She didn't argue. It'd be worthless, so she changed the subject. "Julie would enjoy the frolic at the Kuhns' house. I'll ask her if she wants to join us next Saturday. There's always so much to do, and an extra pair of hands will be welcome, I'm sure. It'll be an easy way to introduce her to the *kinder*."

"Julie? The *Englisch* girl?"

"*Ja*. Remember? I told you last night during supper Philip DeSare has agreed to have Julie spend time with the local *kinder*. She'll be visiting for the first time this afternoon. *Daed* and the boys seemed to think it was a *gut* idea. I thought you did, too, because you didn't say anything then."

"I'm saying something now." *Mamm* gave a sigh that announced she didn't like feeling thwarted by her daughter's calm responses. "I don't know why you offered to do such an absurd thing. Have you forgotten we plain folks are supposed to live separate from the rest of the world?"

"Of course not, but I also remember how many times Jesus told us to love and care for one another."

"What will Rodney think when he hears about your plans?"

Getting a sieve, Aveline dumped the green pods into it. "I'd hope our bishop would *komm* to me and ask me to explain. That he'd understand what I was doing to help a *kind*."

"You don't need to waste your time babysitting an *Englisch* girl." *Mamm* wasn't ready to cede the argument.

"I don't consider it a waste of time." She couldn't hide her astonishment at *Mamm*'s vitriol.

"I tell you bringing that *Englisch* girl here among our own *kinder* is a bad idea."

"Julie is lonely in that big house with no others her own age." She walked into the living room and opened the Bible *Daed* read to them every evening. Turning nearly to the end of the New Testament, she paused when she reached the third chapter of the First Letter of John. She ran her finger down the page and read aloud so *Mamm* couldn't fail to hear in the kitchen, "'But whoso hath this world's good, and seeth his brother have need, and shutteth up his bowels of compassion from him, how dwelleth the love of God in him? My little children, let us not love in word, neither in tongue; but in deed and in truth.'" She closed the Bible, set it on the table by *Daed*'s chair and went into the kitchen.

Mamm folded her arms. "I understand what those verses mean, but I also have seen how putting a fox among the chickens creates chaos."

"Julie isn't a fox. She's a scared *kind* who needs to remember kids aren't supposed to be scared."

When her *mamm* dropped her arms from her angry pose, she said, "This is an unnecessary distraction. I wish you'd put as much effort into finding a husband as you do with this girl."

There it was. *Mamm*'s reason for being bothered by Aveline's hope that she could help Julie. Knowing there was nothing to say that wouldn't upset her *mamm*, she focused on shucking the peas. *Mamm*'s gaze drilled into her, but Aveline acted as if she were unaware of the cloud of frustration hanging in the kitchen.

When *Mamm* stormed out of the kitchen, letting the door slam behind her, Aveline gripped the edges of the sink and sent up a quick prayer for guidance. Quarreling with *Mamm* wasn't something she ever wanted to do, but she couldn't let *Mamm*'s obsession with finding her a husband keep Aveline from helping a wounded *kind* to heal.

And herself as well.

Mamm said nothing to Aveline during the midday meal. Aveline wondered if either of her brothers or *Daed* noticed. They monopolized the conversation with making plans for harvesting the few acres of potatoes they'd planted while waiting for the calves to be born in the spring and to decide where they'd sell their small harvest.

"Why not put a stand out front?" asked Wes, whose hair was a brighter red than Aveline's. She guessed when he married and began to grow his beard, it would be sparse and a surprising blond, like his whiskers. "Let people *komm* and buy what they want when they want."

Dwayne was insistent they should check first to see if Mattie Kuhns would sell their potatoes at the Celtic Hill Farm Shop. "One and done," he said, clapping his palms together as if knocking dirt off them. He stood a head taller than his older brother and his blond hair had already begun to recede at his temples and his crown. "That would give us time to work on the fences, so we can move the herd behind the barn."

They debated those points, with *Daed* adding his opinion while *Mamm* tried to get them to talk about how ungrateful Aveline was. She used the phrase "unnecessary distraction" twice. Aveline thanked God her brothers and *Daed* kept talking about the harvest.

Daed gave her a wink as he went out the door, and Aveline hid her smile. *Mamm* wouldn't appreciate learning they'd colluded against her during the meal. Aveline vowed to make *Mamm*'s favorite peach upside-down cake tomorrow to atone for playing an unknowing part in the conspiracy.

When Aveline picked up the basket of cookies she'd baked to send with Julie to her *daed*, *Mamm* made another snide comment about wasting her time with *Englischers*. Aveline left without replying. It wouldn't have mattered what she said. Anything would have been wrong except for announcing a man had asked her to be his wife.

"How are you doing?" asked *Daed* as she passed him along the lane.

"Fine."

"Your *mamm* is looking out for what's best for you. She loves you, you know."

"I know." She smiled, understanding what he wasn't saying. "I love her. You, too, *Daed*."

"You're a *gut* daughter." He didn't add anything else as he headed toward the barn with his easy stride.

Aveline walked in the other direction. Her basket swung as she let the tension roll off her shoulders. Keeping an eye out for reporters and happy not to see any, she strolled along the road. The early August sunshine was pleasant, not as hot and laced with humidity as in Ontario. She didn't think of that province often. Her home was in Prince Edward Island, and she loved the rugged land and the outwardly tough but kind-hearted people.

She heard her name called when she neared a mailbox labeled Overgard. The name belonged to Lucas's sister-in-law's late first husband. Because the family intended to move to Juan's farm as soon as the construction on the bungalow there was completed, no one had bothered to update the name on the mailbox.

When she saw Lucas using his straw hat to get her attention, she smiled. She turned down the lane to meet him and found herself admiring his strong shoulders. He was so handsome with his dark eyes and even darker hair. No wonder the other women hadn't been able to resist throwing themselves at him. How vexed *Mamm* had been when Aveline hadn't joined that bevy, vying for his attention! *Mamm*'s scold had been the impetus for Aveline to flirt with his cousin Mark, ruining any chance Aveline had had to become better friends with his now-wife Kirsten.

The heat of humiliation seared through her, and she hoped it wasn't visible on her face as she got closer to Lucas.

It must have been hidden because he smiled as he greeted her and added, "Did you notice? Not a single reporter in sight."

"I did notice that. I hope they're gone for *gut*."

"A few are lingering by my farm. That's why I had Randall drop Julie off here."

"There aren't any at our place."

"I'm glad to hear that." He gave her that naughty-boy grin. "I may have encouraged the police to mention water buffalo can be tremendously dangerous if they get out."

"That's not true!"

"You know that, and so do I. If the reporters do some research, they'll know it, too. Until then, they're keeping their distance."

She laughed. "I've got to say it's was an inspired idea not to bring Julie to your house or mine," she said as they continued toward the white farmhouse.

When they passed the simple stand where Annalise sold her wooden boats and coasters and horses, Lucas paused. "Doing that was Juan's idea, because he hasn't been happy about reporters coming here either."

"They came here?"

"Once." He explained how Annalise had used the excuse of something in the oven to avoid revealing the truth.

"They bought it?" she asked.

"They did, because it was the truth." He chuckled. "Annalise sold them a bunch of things, so many, she's asked Juan to delay making any plans to move her workshop to his farm."

"Let us know if she needs any help with that."

An odd expression crossed his face before his usual smile reappeared. "I'm sure Annalise will put out a call for help."

Aveline didn't respond to what he *hadn't* said. She didn't like to think of her *mamm* as a pariah in their community, but she couldn't ignore the truth. How many times had she seen people drift away from a group as soon as *Mamm* had joined it?

To say nothing seemed wrong. She wanted to follow the Commandments and honor her parents. She must not pick and choose which verses to live by, and the ninth one required her not to bear false witness. She couldn't pretend Chalonna Lampel was anything she wasn't. Treading that fine line was becoming a greater challenge each day, and she was grateful for *Daed*'s kind words earlier. She needed to act as he did. Hold on to the family's love for one another and concentrate on what a gift that was from God.

So instead of defending *Mamm* or confirming Lucas's opinion, she said, "*Mamm* told Mattie we would be there to help with the frolic to prepare for church next week."

"Benjamin is having a frolic the same day to thin out his wood lot before the snows come and take down branches. Both of them will appreciate the help." He leaned toward her and lowered his voice, though there was nobody else near. "Don't tell anyone, but Mattie may be making her amazing chocolate cake with coconut frosting."

"That sounds delicious."

"It is." He grinned. "You've never had any of it?"

"Not that I recall."

"You *would* recall if you'd had a single bite. I tell you, if the Israelites had had her chocolate cake instead of manna, they would gladly have kept wandering through the desert for another forty years."

Aveline laughed, grateful for his teasing. Though he hadn't said, she could tell he'd guessed something was bothering her. That he hadn't probed was a relief.

The back door opened, and three small forms and a large one raced toward them. For a second, Aveline almost believed it was Moobeam coming for a treat. Then she saw the creature wasn't quite as big, and she knew it was the Saint Bernard mix with the improbable name of Susie. In her wake was a black pug they called Mei-Mei, along with two girls.

Julie held the hand of the smaller blond girl who whisked a white cane in front of her. She was Evie Overgard, Lucas's four-year-old niece. For the first time since they'd discovered Julie, the *kind* was giggling.

"Evie has two dogs!" she shouted with excitement. "She says I can play with them."

"Sounds like fun, ain't so?" Aveline grinned, as well, delighted by the change in Julie so soon after her arrival.

Herding the lot toward the rear porch, Aveline opened her basket and offered the *kinder* and Lucas the cookies. The two dogs gave her forlorn looks. She found a cookie with no chocolate chips and broke it into pieces. She was rewarded with happy doggy faces.

"These ares *gut*," Evie said, brushing crumbs

off her dress. Turning to Julie, she asked, "Cans I touches your face?"

Julie hesitated, then bent so the smaller girl could run her fingers over her features. She jerked back, giggling. "That tickles!"

"Does it?" Aveline asked before Evie could speak. Seeing the hurt expression on the little girl's face, Aveline knew pointing it out might upset the *kind*.

"Evie's fingers feel like bugs on my skin," Julie declared.

"Not bugs!" Evie protested.

"No, not bugs." Aveline put a hand on each girl's shoulder. "Butterflies."

"Oooo," Julie murmured. "I like butterflies. They're so pretty."

"They've got the lightest touch. I wonder if their toes tickle the flowers."

The two girls dissolved into giggles at the thought. Evie restarted her examination of Julie's face. Though Julie tried to hold still, she kept flinching from what they began to call "butterfly kisses."

As soon as Evie was done, Julie asked to touch the younger girl's features. It was Evie's turn to twist her mouth and laugh.

"Hey!" Julie cried. "You told me not to laugh."

"I'm trying not to but..." She giggled harder, saying, "Julie, I likes your face."

"I like yours, too." Abruptly, she asked, "Do you have more dogs?"

"Just two. *Grossmammi* Fern's pug and my Susie. She's bigger."

Julie laughed. "A whole lot bigger."

Lucas sat on the edge of the porch and had the pug on his lap. Petting the black dog, he asked, "Julie, did you know Susie used to be afraid of Mei-Mei?"

That brought more amused grins from the girls.

Aveline's gaze was caught by Lucas's, and she was pleased—and puzzled—to see he had the same reaction to Julie acting like a normal *kind* instead of a traumatized one. He was smiling like a teenager getting his first buggy. Who was the real Lucas Kuepfer? The flirtatious man who didn't seem to care how many hearts he broke or the man who was so excited to see a *kind*'s heart heal?

"Do you have other animals?" Julie asked the younger girl.

"Not lots, but *Daed* Juan gots plenty, and *Onkel* Lucas gots more. He's gots goats."

"Goats?" Julie's eyes lit as she looked at Lucas. "Can we go see them?"

"Not today," he replied, his smile wavering.

"Why not?"

When he looked in her direction, this time

with an unspoken request for help, Aveline said, "The goats are resting. You know how cats like to catnap? Goats like to—"

"Goat-nap?" Julie interrupted with the same enthusiasm she'd showed with Evie.

"You guessed it." She was grateful she hadn't had to lie or to be truthful and explain how she and Lucas hoped Julie would remain out of sight and safe. The girl seemed satisfied with her response, which was a relief. "We'll see them when they're awake. Ain't so, Lucas?"

"*Ja*," he said, his smile returning. "Evie, you should show Julie your room before you start packing to move to Juan's farm."

"First," Julie said, "Evie wants to find out what Aveline looks like."

"You haven't touched Aveline's face before?" Lucas couldn't hide his amazement.

Heat climbed Aveline's cheeks. How could she explain she'd never said more than a greeting to the Overgards after church services? So often, she had to hurry home to check on the herd. The cows had been pregnant for almost eleven months, and then the young calves demanded her attention. It had been a *gut* excuse to avoid the young men her *mamm* chose. Belatedly, she realized how much she'd missed. Her neighbors didn't know her. If she'd made an effort to ignore *Mamm*'s schemes, she might not have embarrassed herself by flirting so outrageously with Lucas's cousin.

She cut her eyes toward Lucas. She hoped her face hadn't betrayed her thoughts. When she realized he was focused on the *kinder*, she saw the kindhearted man who contradicted his heartless reputation.

Evie tilted her head as she considered Julie's question. "No, I haves not touched Aveline's face. Not yet."

"You should," the other girl urged. "She's pretty."

"Prettier than my *mamm*?"

It was Julie's turn to ponder before she answered, making Aveline wonder if a concern about finding the right words was something that could be inherited. The girl's pause was so much like something her *daed* would do.

"Both are pretty." Julie looked puzzled. "Even if they don't wear makeup, like some of the women who come to our house. You can't see their skin because they've put so much stuff on their faces." She took Evie's hand and moved her thumb and first finger about a few centimeters apart. "That much."

"It doesn't drips off their faces?"

"No. I think it hardens like concrete."

Aveline couldn't keep from chuckling at the *kinder* who were being so serious.

Evie faced her. "Does it gets like concrete, Aveline?"

"I don't know. I've never worn cosmetics."

"Me neither." Evie bobbed her chin to emphasize her words. "Susie wills not either."

"Dogs don't wear makeup," Julie said.

"Never?"

"Not that I've ever heard of." A hint of uncertainty sifted into her words.

Putting a hand on each girl's shoulder, Aveline said, "Animals are beautiful just the way God created them. As you two girls are."

"Aveline, okay to touchs?" asked Evie.

"I think it's long overdue. Don't you?"

Lucas almost answered Aveline's question, then realized it was posed to the *kinder*. When she sat on the porch so her face was level with Evie's, he rested his shoulder against one of the roof supports, making sure he stood between the *kinder* and the road. He wished Evie would take Julie inside and away from any chance sighting by one of the persistent reporters, but an appraising glance told him that as long as he stood there, nobody on the road would be able to see Aveline and the girls.

Aveline took Evie's hands and drew them toward her face. "Go ahead, Evie."

"Don't laughs."

"I'll try not to."

The *kind*'s face tightened with concentration as her fingertips ran over Aveline's features. Lucas was astonished by the flood of envy that swelled over him as he wished his fingers were touching Aveline's skin. He yearned to slide his own fingers along the contours of her face and across her parted lips. Which would be softer? Her skin or her eyelashes that curled against her cheeks?

When he realized he was slanting toward Aveline, he cleared his throat and pushed himself back. "Evie, one thing your fingers won't show you are her freckles."

"What ares freckles?" the little girl asked.

"Spots," Julie said.

"You've gots spots?" Evie asked. "Dos other people gots spots? Nobody tolds me about spots."

Lucas put a calming hand on the *kind*'s shoulder. "Some people have freckles. Some don't. Freckles are on someone's cheeks. Imagine this." He touched Evie's face. "Spots here on one cheek and more on the other cheek."

"I don'ts understands."

With a smile and wink at Julie, he said, "Imagine this instead. If you blew a handful of dirt toward her, the specks would stick to her skin."

"Ugh," Aveline said at the same time as the

girls before adding, "What a horrible idea! I don't have a dirty face."

"I didn't say you did. I was trying to explain to Evie what freckles are."

Aveline took Evie's hands in hers. "My *grossmammi* always said someone scattered a thimble of cinnamon on my face when I was a *boppli*. That's why the spots are everywhere."

"Why you ares sweet?" the little girl asked.

Giving her a hug, Aveline said, "Maybe I needed sweetening. You don't have any freckles, and you're as sweet as fudge."

"Fudge!" Evie grinned. "Julie, lets makes fudge."

Without another word, both girls rushed into the house.

Silence fell between Lucas and Aveline who came to her feet and brushed cookie crumbs off her dress. He took a single step toward her, but she was up the steps and into the house, the door closing behind her, before he could get a single word out.

What had happened? He usually was so glib with any woman he'd met, a skill he'd honed since he arrived in Prince Edward Island.

The answer was simple.

Aveline wasn't like any other woman he'd ever met.

Chapter Nine

"Will Evie ever be able to see like I do, Lucas?" Julie asked as her *daed*'s car turned into the lane at Lucas's farm later the next week.

Lucas glanced from Aveline to where his brother was walking Evie and the two dogs, one large and one small, back home. Nothing but the complete truth would suffice. The youngsters had already become close. Though Evie was plain and Julie was *Englisch* and there was four years difference in their ages, the two girls had found common ground in their love of animals and their pain at having lost a parent at a young age. They'd insisted on coming to Lucas's farm to admire his goats and try to catch them napping. Neither of them suspected Aveline had spun them a tall tale.

Glad Evie was out of earshot so he could speak without being concerned about upsetting his niece,

Lucas said, "Some *doktors* have told her family no, that she won't ever see as we do."

"That's so sad." Tears bubbled into Julie's eyes.

"It is," Aveline interjected, not looking in his direction. She didn't need to. He could discern how vexed she was by his answer. Her annoyance was undercurrent in her voice as she said, "Julie, we need to remember *doktors* aren't always right. There's a procedure that may bring her a little sight."

"That's true," Lucas said. "It's a long shot, so nobody knows if it'll help, but God may inspire someone to devise a way to make it possible for Evie to see as we do. Nothing is impossible with God."

"Then she wouldn't have to touch our faces to discover what we look like."

"That's right." Lucas took a moment before asking, "Did it bother you when Evie traced her fingers along your face?"

"No, but it tickled, and she kept telling me not to crinkle my nose when I laughed."

"Every motion distorts your face a bit."

Aveline added, "Evie needs to get an image to hold in her mind."

"That makes sense." Julie paused as the car stopped near them. Opening the door, she got in.

Lucas started to close the door, but Randall emerged from the vehicle and halted him. The chauffeur held out a folded piece of paper. "Mr. DeSare is hoping you'd be able to come over to the house for a short visit, Mr. Kuepfer."

"Call me Lucas," he said.

Randall nodded. "Can you meet with Mr. De-Sare?" He looked at Aveline. "You, too, if you've got the time."

Opening the folded page, Lucas saw the note echoed what Randall had already asked. He handed it to Aveline as he checked the height of the sun. It was already close to the western horizon, spreading its rays across the river like an imaginary bridge. It wasn't time yet to milk, and supper could wait.

"Let's go," he said to the chauffeur. "Or, at least, I can go. Aveline, do you need to head home?"

He wasn't sure how she'd answer. All afternoon, Aveline had been uneasy in his company. He knew something had changed between them...and not for the better.

"Not right away," she replied. "I'm sure Philip is curious how the day went, and if we can help him and Julie, we must."

"I agree."

She gave him a frown, and he wondered if his voice had been too enthusiastic. Knowing anything he said would make the situation more uncomfortable, he reached to reopen the door. He was surprised when she walked around to the passenger's-side door.

Randall shot him a sympathetic grin, and Lucas ducked into the car before the chauffeur spoke. He didn't need to see the other man's pity. He already felt pitiful enough.

Julie squealed with delight as she looked from him to Aveline. "You're coming with me?"

"*Ja*," Lucas said as he slid in and closed the door.

"Can Evie come, too?"

"Not tonight, but we can talk to your *daed* about her visiting you at home sometime."

Aveline frowned over the girl's head, and he realized he was speaking out of turn. It was Philip's place to extend an invitation, not Lucas's to ask for one.

He was relieved he didn't have to say anything because Julie chattered, filling the car with her excitement about a possible visit from Evie and the dogs to her house. Though he had no idea if the *Englischer* would welcome two rambunctious dogs, he doubted Philip would deny his daughter the chance to spend time with her new friends.

"I wish Daddy wouldn't send his security guys to follow me around," Julie said, annoyed.

"What?" asked Aveline before he could.

"I don't like them hanging around."

"Hanging around?" Aveline glanced at him, worry in her eyes. "Where?"

"In the woods at Evie's house." The girl picked at a snag on her jeans. "And near the road by your farm, Lucas."

"I didn't see anyone," he said.

"You're not supposed to." The *kind* gave a shrug. "I'm surprised he let me see him."

"What's he look like?"

"A guy. Dark clothes. Like the guys Daddy has watching the house. I don't like them hanging around."

Aveline asked, "Have you mentioned that to your *daed*?"

"He gets upset when I do." Her mouth straightened. "I don't like upsetting him."

"Would you like us to mention it to him?" Lucas wanted to retract the question as soon as he asked it. Getting involved in the *Englischers'* lives would make a complicated situation more difficult. Yet how could he turn his back on a *kind* in need?

He asked that question aloud after he and Aveline had gotten out of the car and were walking toward the DeSares' house. Julie had run ahead, and Randall was parking the vehicle near the garages.

"You can't turn away," Aveline said. "At least, I can't."

"*Danki* for understanding."

"I wish *Mamm* would." She wiped her hands against her black apron as he reached to open the door Julie had left ajar in her wake.

"What doesn't she understand?"

A warm flush climbed her face, swallowing her adorable freckles. Her voice was a whisper when she replied, "She thinks I should be thinking more about my future *kinder* than someone else's *kind*."

"My *grossmammi* used to say that worry wastes today and masks tomorrow's opportunities…" He didn't want to continue the adage and wondered why he'd started it.

She finished it. "By confusing them with yesterday's regrets. *Danki* for reminding me of that saying."

"I hope it helps." It wasn't helping him to recall his own shame. He knew he should toss it aside like weeds in his fields and live the life God had given him, but it clung to him like a burr. It pricked at him each time he made a decision, refusing to be ignored.

Lucas walked with Aveline into the grand house. A maid motioned for them to enter the big room with the marvelous views of the dunes and the sea.

Philip stood, putting papers on a table by his chair. He greeted them and urged each to sit. Offering them *kaffi*, he waited until they'd added *millich* and sugar before leaning back in his chair.

"Thanks for coming over," the *Englischer* said. "I know harvest time is almost upon you, so I thought I'd ask before you're up to your ears in potatoes."

Smiling, because he knew that was what the other man hoped he'd do, Lucas said, "Up to my ears would be a *gut* thing."

"How does the harvest look this year?"

"The weather has been cooperative, so we're expecting a crop at least as big as last year's."

"Glad to hear it." Philip didn't take a breath before he began to ask how Julie was doing on her visits.

Lucas let Aveline answer the questions about how the days had gone because Philip aimed each of them at her. In fact, Lucas wasn't sure why he'd been invited to the house.

At a pause in the conversation, he said, "There's one other thing, Philip. Julie has told us she doesn't like having security follow her to our farms."

"Nobody's been following Julie anywhere." Philip set down his cup and leaned forward to refill it. His pose was casual. His tone was not. "I ended my contract with the security company last week. They weren't doing anything other than stopping tourists walking on the beach. I realized I was making things worse rather than better because I didn't want us to live in an armed compound."

"Does Julie know that you don't have security any longer?"

"We have security. Cameras and the regular staff, but not the guys patrolling the property." He took a sip then put his cup on the table. "I plan to tell her, but I haven't yet. I didn't want her scared."

"She's scared anyhow. She thinks someone is watching her."

"Why would she think that?"

"Because she's seen someone watching her."

Philip's face grew taut but relaxed as Julie came from the kitchen with a plate of cupcakes. His hands on his lap remained in fists while he donned a smile for his daughter. The man was a *gut* actor, keeping his true feelings off his face, but Lucas could tell Philip DeSare was furious the threat to his daughter might not have gone away.

That was why Lucas was amazed when Philip agreed to have Julie join Aveline for the work frolic at his cousin Mattie's house in two days. He comprehended the battle within the *Englischer* when, an hour later, Philip drew him aside while Julie went outside to walk Aveline to the waiting car and talk about her next visit.

"Don't let her out of your sight," Philip pleaded.

"She's safe with our community," Lucas replied, putting his hand on the other man's arm. "I'm glad you're okay with letting her join us. She and Evie are eager to go to the work frolic Saturday."

"I'm not sure I'd say I was okay with her going, but I can't keep her locked in her room. I've never seen her as happy as she's been in the past week."

"We'll make sure one of us is with her all the time. You can trust us."

Philip sighed. "I know I can trust you, though I'm not sure who else I can."

"Your staff—"

"I trust them, or they wouldn't be here. I haven't let anyone I don't trust into the house since the incident." He offered his hand to Lucas. "Thank you for helping."

"We're glad to."

"I know you are." Philip glanced at where Aveline and Julie stood by the tabletop fountain. He clapped Lucas on the shoulder, then called to his daughter. "C'mon, Julie. Let's go for a swim before my next meeting." Lowering his voice, he looked at Aveline, who was hugging the girl. "You two are a great team. You belong together. Don't ever forget that."

Lucas almost asked the other man what he meant, then realized he'd be better off not to.

He might hear what his heart had been begging him to heed: Aveline was becoming a vital part of every beat it took.

Mattie Kuhns was the only woman among the four cousins who'd risked everything to find their dreams in Prince Edward Island. While her cousins had purchased farms, fulfilling a dream of having their own land, she and her younger sister, Daisy, had bought a beat-up Quonset hut and rebuilt it into a popular farm shop. It'd been open for two summers and attracted customers from as far as Summerside, three-quarters of the way across the Island.

She was no taller than Aveline, and golden hair was visible beneath her pleated *kapp*. She smiled and welcomed Aveline and Julie into the house that she and her husband, Benjamin, had spent the past year renovating while they'd worked at their shops. Now it was filled with color, conversation and laughter.

"Buckets and brooms are in the kitchen or on the porch," Mattie said as they stepped inside. "Or grab a dust cloth and shoo dust out the door."

"*Komm mol*, Julie." Aveline took the girl's hand and led her on a winding path past where others were already at work. "What would you like to do?"

"I don't know." The *kind* scanned the two

rooms that looked like a beehive as each woman and girl worked on her individual job. "I don't know how to do any of the things they're doing."

"How about I get us cloths? We can dust the top of the floor molding."

"I don't know how."

Remembering how Philip had said his daughter did chores at home, Aveline had to wonder if she did or if one of the DeSares' many servants took care of the tasks.

"Who are you?" asked a young voice from behind them.

Aveline turned to see Daisy Albrecht, Mattie's nearly sixteen-year-old sister. Daisy sat in her wheelchair along with the battered doll she called Boppi Lynn. The doll was always with Daisy who had Down syndrome.

"This is Julie DeSare," Aveline replied, seeing Julie was shy with the forthright Daisy.

"You're *Englisch*."

"I'm Canadian!" asserted the girl.

"Me, too!" Daisy grinned. "And so is Boppi Lynn. Boppi Lynn likes you. I do, too."

Aveline didn't bother to explain that, to the Amish, everyone else was *Englisch*. Daisy had handled it fine on her own.

"Ah, here you are," Mattie said as she came over to check on her effusive sister. "You've met Julie? *Gut*."

"We're going to be friends, ain't so, Julie?" asked Daisy.

Julie smiled. "I'd like that. I like having friends. I'm friends with Evie. Do you know her?"

"*Ja*. We're cousins."

"Oh, I wish I had cousins."

"I've got lots, so you can be one, too." She looked up at Aveline. "That's okay, ain't so?"

Aveline nodded. "I think that's a *wunderbaar* idea. You can be real friends and honorary cousins. How does that sound?"

"Great!" Julie said at the same time Daisy said, "*Wunderbaar!*"

Mattie turned to answer a quick question from another volunteer at the frolic, then said, "I hope you can stay long enough to say hi to Benjamin."

"How's he doing?" Aveline asked.

"He's happy." Her fingers lingered on her abdomen, and Aveline recalled the rumors that Mattie was pregnant. "He loves having time to carve and build clocks. His business is growing. At first, most of his customers were plain folks."

Daisy giggled. "We knew who was walking out together before families and friends did. Lots of the fellows like to buy a clock for their future wife as a birthday or Christmas present."

Mattie wagged a playful finger at her youngest sister. "Remember what we said about keeping secrets?"

"It's important when telling would ruin a surprise." Daisy winked at them.

Aveline smiled but Julie remained serious as she said, "I don't like secrets. That man kept saying I needed to be quiet, that if I revealed where we were, it'd be horrible for me."

No one spoke for a long minute. Aveline guessed the others were as worried as she was about saying the wrong thing and making the *kind* feel worse.

Daisy broke the tension by linking her arm through Julie's. "Boppi Lynn says you're the bravest person she knows."

"She does?" Julie's eyes lost their haunted dullness.

"Ask her yourself." Daisy held up the plastic doll. Its painted face had faded from the many kisses Daisy had given her constant companion.

"Boppi Lynn—"

"She likes to be held when you talk to her." Daisy pushed the doll toward Julie's hands.

Aveline swallowed her gasp when she saw the astonishment in Mattie's eyes. Had Mattie's sister ever let someone else take her beloved doll?

Julie cradled the battered doll in her arms. Looking into the doll's eyes that no longer opened and closed, she said, "I'm Julie."

Daisy chided, "She knows who you are. Boppi Lynn is smart."

"*Ja*," Aveline interjected, "she is. Very smart."

Mattie wore a tenuous smile, but her gaze never left her sister and the doll in Julie's arms.

"Thank you for thinking I'm brave, Boppi Lynn," Julie whispered. "I don't always feel brave."

"Neither does Boppi Lynn," Daisy said in a consoling tone, sounding much older than her fifteen years.

"Aveline is the brave one." Julie looked at her.

"Not always." Aveline stroked the girl's hair that was already coming out of her barrettes.

Julie put the doll in her arms. "Boppi Lynn and I think you're the bravest person we know."

"*Danki*, but I was where I was because Moobeam was a bad girl that day." She handed the doll to Daisy who was holding out her hands.

"Bad calf," Daisy said, "but you're a *gut* girl, Boppi Lynn." She cuddled her doll close before grasping Julie's fingers and saying, "Let's go and check the oven. Mattie and I are making cookies."

The mention of cookies brought a brighter smile from Julie. She hurried after Daisy, who cut her way through the crowd with ease.

Aveline was going to say something to Mattie but their hostess was called away. Grabbing a cloth off a pile on a nearby table, Aveline began to clean the faint smudge of dust off the molding in front of her.

She kept an eye on Julie, who remained by Daisy's side as they offered warm cookies to the workers. Cleaning the low moldings was easy, though a rumble of pain began to resonate at the base of her spine. She straightened and put her hand against her back. Another delicious cookie would be the best way to remedy the twinges.

As she reached the door to the kitchen, Aveline heard an angry voice announce, "I don't trust her."

"You don't know Aveline." That voice belonged to Mattie.

"I know enough!" retorted the woman she couldn't identify only by her voice.

Aveline backed away. She shouldn't be eavesdropping. How many times had *Daed* reminded her that what other people thought or said about her was none of her business? *Mamm* would say if Aveline listened when others didn't know she was there, she was sure to hear the truth. A painful truth.

This time she had to agree with *Mamm*.

She took another step, then halted when she realized if she moved any farther, she'd be visible through the door. Not certain where the two women stood in the kitchen, she couldn't risk them discovering her listening to their conversation. She considered walking casually past without looking in their direction. She could use a determined stride that would suggest her mind was on her next task.

If she could pull it off…

She wasn't ready to test it. On the other hand, she couldn't just remain where she was. Someone was sure to wonder why she was doing a statue impersonation and ask her if everything was okay. That question would be heard by Mattie and the other woman, and the end result would be the same as if she'd jumped into the kitchen and cried, "Aha! Look at me!"

"You've heard the rumors, Mattie." The no-nonsense tone dragged Aveline's attention back to the conversation.

Rumors? Which rumors? Aveline bit her lip to silence the questions.

"I hear lots of rumors, Kirsten," Mattie answered.

Aveline pressed her hand to her throat that seemed so clogged she couldn't breathe. Kirsten was married to Mark Yutzy, the man Aveline had flirted with when *Mamm* had insisted. Aveline had been foolish to inveigle an invitation from Mark to a benefit supper, and she'd avoided him and Kirsten since then.

"I hear some that are true," Mattie went on, "but I hear a lot that aren't."

"Don't act as if you don't care. I know you do.

The talk about Lucas and Aveline Lampel planning to get married has got to have you upset."

Planning to get married? Who would believe such a daft story? From what Aveline had heard, Kirsten had a *gut* head on her shoulders. Why would she give any credence to such a tale? Someone who thought Aveline was so desperate to marry that she'd set her sights on the man in their community who flirted with women but hadn't ever been serious about one. It wasn't logical, but Kirsten wasn't being rational.

"Lucas's life is his own." Mattie's tone remained calm.

It didn't ease her cousin-in-law's outrage. "Do you want him to marry into *that* family? I don't."

Aveline had to get away. She couldn't listen to the venom being spouted by a woman who had every reason to despise her. She took a single step, blinded by her own tears.

And ran into someone else. Dashing away the tears, she stared at Kirsten, a beautiful brunette.

"I—I—I didn't mean to eavesdrop," she managed to say.

Mattie gave her a bolstering smile, but Kirsten crossed her arms and frowned. She didn't believe Aveline.

Knowing she wasn't going to get through to Kirsten by beating around the bush, Aveline said, "It's true. I was planning to have another cookie, and I heard voices in the kitchen. When I realized you were talking about me, I wanted to move away, but I didn't know how I could without you seeing me."

"Sor—" Mattie began.

Aveline cut her off. "No, don't apologize. I have let Kirsten's bad feelings fester for too long. I need to be honest as I should have been months ago."

"I can leave if you'd like to talk privately," Mattie said.

Aveline shook her head. "No, I'd like you to stay if Kirsten is okay with that."

The brunette nodded, but her face remained unreadable. No doubt she was distressed her comments had been overheard.

Aveline pushed aside that thought. Spying on them would have been, in Kirsten's opinion, the least of her sins. "I should have asked your forgiveness back then," she said with a sigh. "To be honest, I was so embarrassed by the whole thing with Mark, I found it difficult to talk about it."

"That, I understand." Kirsten's voice remained chilly.

"I did implore Mark to ask me to go with him to the benefit supper. My excuse is—"

"You didn't know we were becoming serious about each other."

"No, I knew—"

Kirsten's dark brows rose. "You knew?" She whirled to Mattie. "Did you hear that?"

"I did," said Mattie, looking from her cousin's wife to Aveline. "I'm not sure what Aveline means."

"I mean," Aveline quickly replied, grateful for Mattie's intervention, "my excuse is I knew I needed to convince my *mamm* I was making an effort to find a husband." She hurried on when Kirsten opened her mouth to retort. "It was a sad happenstance Mark was the first guy I saw after *Mamm* insisted I prove to her I didn't need her help in selecting a husband. I was desperate to get her off my back, so I acted like a fool. I'm sorry if I hurt you and him. So very, very sorry. I'm also sorry I didn't tell you this months ago."

Neither woman spoke for a long minute. Mattie put a hand on Aveline's arm and gave her a smile. An understanding one that Aveline was grateful to see.

Mattie's words, however, were for Kirsten. "Now you know the other side of the story."

For a long moment, Kirsten didn't say anything. Sighing, she said, "I'm going to be as blunt as you were. I know your *mamm* isn't the easiest person to be around." She faltered. "I should have asked you why you acted as you did instead of listening to rumors and jumping to conclusions."

"Rumors I'm desperate to find a man to marry.

That I don't care who it is as long as he's out of the cradle and not yet in the ground."

Kirsten's lips twitched. "*Ja*, though not in those exact words." She sighed and began, "You and Lucas…"

"What about us?"

"Is there an 'us' with the two of you?"

"*Ja* and no." She sighed. "There is an 'us' in that we're waiting to hear what the bishop has to say about the reward Philip DeSare offered us. There is an 'us' in trying to help Philip's daughter. There is no 'us' when it comes to having our wedding date published. We're friends and neighbors."

"Nothing more?" Kirsten asked.

"No." Regret careened through her, but she ignored it. Now wasn't the time to wonder why Lucas found every woman except her fascinating enough to flirt with.

Chapter Ten

That Sunday after the church service had ended, Lucas walked out of the Kuhns' house and stretched. A lifetime of sitting on backless benches should have prepared him for the longer than usual service this morning. There had been a lot of announcements about events after the harvest, including an auction at the end of October to raise money to have a school built. The scholars had gathered last spring in a patched polytunnel behind Mattie's farm shop, but it was time for a permanent building. Juan and Annalise had donated land for the school, and the community would provide the labor. The auction funds would help pay for the materials they already had on order.

He'd listened through the announcements for Aveline's brothers' weddings to be published, but Wes later told him that wouldn't happen for another month. Lucas wanted to know the dates because, during the next fortnight of preparations, Aveline wouldn't have any time to spend with Julie.

Was the little girl right that someone was watching her? He didn't want to believe it, but Julie was honest about everything else. The fact also remained that Trace hadn't appeared smart enough to figure the abduction out on his own.

Lucas hadn't had a chance to ask Aveline if she had new insight into the enigma. Today would be a *gut* day to find out what she was thinking. Julie wasn't visiting, so he and Aveline could find a quiet spot and discuss the situation. *If you go off with her somewhere alone, everyone is going to talk.* He shuddered at the thought. Changing his reputation was something he'd wanted to do, but adding to the already virulent whispers he and Aveline were walking out together wasn't the way.

He almost laughed aloud. If the gossips had any idea how seldom he'd been alone with Aveline, they'd be shocked silent. Or almost silent, which might be the best anyone could hope for. He swallowed a chuckle. Was it possible the longest he and Aveline had been alone together had been when they'd been searching for her rambling water buffalo calf before finding Julie?

All yearning to laugh fled. He tried to tell himself it was for the best because he would have been a fool to risk his heart. Yet he was intrigued by the woman she was, not the woman gossip had painted her.

"There you are," Juan said as he walked with care toward Lucas. Though his sight had mostly returned, he wore thick glasses and continued to use a cane to guide him on uneven ground.

His younger brother wasn't alone. Their cousin Mark walked alongside Juan. Mark's property abutted Lucas's farm. Before planting their potato crop that spring, he and Mark had taken down the fences between a couple of their fields. Already, Lucas knew they'd be pulling out more after the harvest. He'd been amazed by the time they saved not having to turn their draft teams at each fence. They'd been able to continue the long rows without a break and gained at least a half dozen hills in each row. A small addition to their profits, but every penny counted as they built their futures.

"I thought you'd want to know how the meeting went," Juan said.

"The meeting with Aveline's *daed* and the bishop?"

His brother nodded. "If our places were reversed, I'd be so curious I would have been listening at the window."

"Me, too," Mark said as he leaned his hand on a nearby tree.

"So tell me," Lucas replied, not wanting to admit his thoughts had been on Aveline and not the reward Philip had insisted they accept. "What was decided?"

"Nothing," his brother said.

"Nothing?"

"Nothing." Juan shook his head in disgust. "Everyone agrees Philip is right when he says he can't renege on the reward, but everyone also agrees it wouldn't be right for you to accept it."

"Where does that leave us?"

Juan grimaced. "Right where we were. Rodney wants to meet with Julie's *daed* and discuss it further."

"At this rate," Mark said, "the paper the checks are written on will crumble away before anyone decides anything."

Lucas didn't answer. When he and Aveline had decided they couldn't accept the reward, he hadn't imagined it'd create such a to-do. There must be a simple solution. Something they'd overlooked in their determination to do what was right for everyone involved.

The others must have guessed he didn't want to talk about the reward any longer because Mark said, "Mattie wants to know, before you leave, if you'd like to take leftover food home with you for supper tonight."

"Who said I was leaving?"

"You always do right after the midday meal is over."

Did he? Lucas realized he'd developed a habit of heading home as soon as possible. To avoid being with other people. Nobody would believe garrulous Lucas Kuepfer wanted time alone with his thoughts.

"There were rumors," Juan said, "you're thinking of leaving the Island because you aren't happy here."

"Nothing could be further from the truth," Lucas replied, trying to remember the last time he'd been happy. His mind answered with an image of Aveline smiling at him and laughing at something he'd said.

"Glad to hear that," Mark said with a wry grin. "I wouldn't want you to head out and leave me to dig the potatoes on my own."

"You've got your brother to help you."

"Daryn doesn't want to talk about potatoes. He wants to talk about herding cattle and wild horses out west."

Lucas smiled along with the others. Mark's younger brother hadn't ever hidden his dream of becoming a cowboy. Daryn was seventeen, so he was eager to find his way in the world, even if it meant moving far from family.

As Lucas had insisted his brother and cousins do.

Listening while Juan and Mark talked about the upcoming harvest, Lucas glanced around the yard. Where was Aveline? She'd been sitting on the women's side during the service, and he'd seen her go into the kitchen to help Mattie and the other volunteers. Now she was nowhere in sight. He looked at the paddock where the buggy horses waited for their owners to head home. When he saw her horse wasn't among them, he sighed.

"What's wrong?" asked Juan.

Before he could answer, Mark said, "That's a lonesome sigh if I've ever heard one. Why don't you stay here and spend time with us?"

Lucas didn't have an chance to respond before Juan said, "Our company isn't what he's pining for."

"I'm not pining for anything," Lucas asserted.

"Notice," Juan said with a wink, "he said 'anything' not 'anyone.'"

Lucas had heard enough. "Have a *gut* rest of your day. I'm heading home."

"You never said if you wanted Mattie to pack food for you," Mark said.

"I don't need it. Aveline brought over a basket of food yesterday when she and Julie came to see the goats. There's enough to feed the whole district."

"Aveline made the basket?" asked Mark. "Or her *mamm*?"

"I don't know," Lucas replied. "She said she and Julie had been cooking, and they wanted to share what they'd made."

"Be cautious," Juan said, serious. "Her *mamm* is eager for her to be married, and you're a prime target."

Lucas shook his head. "You make me sound like a buck on the first day of hunting season."

"I think you're closer to a wild turkey." He flapped his arms and made a raucous cluck that sounded, to Lucas, like a donkey with laryngitis.

"There aren't any wild turkeys in Prince Edward Island."

Mark raised a brow. "Some have been seen along the roads."

"Tourist birds," Lucas said with a strained grin. "Here for a short visit before they head home."

"Or escapees," Juan said with a chuckle.

"Don't talk to me about escapees."

"Has that water buffalo come to visit your goats again?" his brother asked.

"At least three times. I'm beginning to think Moobeam prefers any company other than her own kind."

"Or she's doing a bit of matchmaking." Mark laughed. "You know how traits run in certain families."

"Bite your tongue!"

His brother and cousin chortled hard before

Juan asked, "Did you consider the calf might not be getting out on her own?"

"*Ja.*" When he saw their shock, he explained what Aveline had told him about finding a gate propped open. "I don't think she's figured out who did it."

"Did she ask her *mamm*?" Mark asked.

"Are you accusing Chalonna of risking their livelihood by allowing the water buffalo to wander along the road and get killed?"

"Of course not." His cousin didn't look as rueful as his words suggested, and Lucas understood why when Mark continued. "Do we know how far Chalonna would go to find her daughter a husband?"

"You're being ridiculous!"

"You're defending Chalonna Lampel, who went to youth events last year to make sure nobody but Dwayne took Estella Gascho home."

"She did? Are you sure, or is this another tale on the Amish grapevine?"

"Daryn saw it."

Lucas wanted to argue Daryn could have misconstrued the situation. When the boy had first arrived to work with Mark, it had been because their parents had thought they needed to get their youngest son away from a group of boys who were a bad influence on him. Daryn had matured a lot since first coming to the Island, and he now could be trusted to make *gut* decisions.

As Lucas needed to do. He'd be putting his life on hold while he mourned losing Robin. Flirting with women meant he didn't have to make a decision about them. Being decisive had once been easy. Now he questioned everything he said and did.

"See you later," he said as he waved to Mark and Juan. He didn't give them time to argue before he walked away.

Ja, he needed to make *gut* decisions…as soon as he figured out what he should do.

The next afternoon, Aveline toted a pail filled with grain across the field to where the water buffalo were gathered, as they often were, by the pond. She emptied the contents into a trough, then reached for the smaller one Julie carried. The girl's eyes were huge as she stared at the large, gentle animals coming toward them.

"Should we run?" Julie asked.

"They won't hurt us." Aveline smiled at the girl.

"They've got horns."

She shook Julie's pail over the trough. Handing it to the *kind*, she said, "Think of them as big puppies."

"With horns!"

"True, and if I want to get Moobeam to behave, I don't say 'sit.'" She lowered her voice as the animals neared. "I say 'treat-treat-treat.'"

"And she obeys?"

"She *tries* to. She'll *komm* over to get a treat, but once when I was telling *Daed* about how she responded, she heard me and broke down the barn door to get her alfalfa cube."

"Wow!"

"*Ja*, wow! That's what Lucas said when I told him the story. You can be sure I never again said those words on the wrong side of the door."

Taking Julie's hand, she drew her away from the trough. The water buffalo were gentle-hearted, but they seemed to forget they were much bigger than Aveline was. A kindly bump from one could knock her off her feet. She didn't want that to happen to Julie, who was already fearful of the herd.

When they were on the other side of the fence with the gate latched, Julie asked, "Which one is Moobeam?"

"Right there." She pointed to the calf trying to nose her way between two of the cows to get a share of the grain. "See the one that's shoving everyone out of her way? That's Moobeam."

"She's so big. I thought she was a calf."

Aveline smiled. "She is. Look at the one next to her. That's her *mamm*. See how big she is."

Julie watched the herd eat. "It's a family."

"*Ja*, it is. We have six cows and three calves, along with the bull." She pointed to the next field. "See that big guy over there? That's the bull."

"He's alone? Isn't he lonely?"

Aveline lowered her voice as if the water buffalo could understand her. "He doesn't like being with the cows when they've got calves."

"Not a nice daddy, huh?"

"The cows care enough to make up for it."

Shaking her head, Julie said, "Calves need a mommy and a daddy."

How could Aveline have let the conversation move in this direction? She'd wanted to amuse Julie, not add to her sorrow.

To distract the girl, Aveline told Julie to look back at the trough. "There are the other two calves. Their names are Mozzar and Rella."

"Like the cheese?"

"*Ja*. My brothers named them that because we plan to use their milk to make mozzarella to sell. My brothers tend to think with their stomachs and taste buds."

Julie giggled. "But you named Moobeam."

"I did. I was going to name her 'Moonbeam' because she was born in the middle of the night, but when I was announcing her name, she gave a loud moo that drowned out my voice. Everyone thought I said, 'Moobeam.' I decided it was a fun name, and it seemed as if the calf had picked it out herself so she must like it, too."

The girl dimpled with delight. "Not any more. Maybe you should change her name to Nanny Goat."

Aveline gave an emoted sigh. "Don't suggest that. She might take it in her head to go over to visit Lucas's goats today."

"Let's go visit them." Julie pushed away from the fence. "C'mon. I want to see Lucas. I haven't seen him in a while."

"It's only been two days since you saw him at Mattie's house." She didn't add that she'd been feeling the same. Though she'd seen Lucas during the church service yesterday—and she hoped he hadn't noted how often she'd glanced in his direction when moving from sitting to kneeling during prayers—she hadn't spoken with him. She'd planned to after lunch, but *Daed* had insisted they leave right after his meeting with Rodney and Juan. A meeting he'd said nothing about.

"He didn't stay long after they finished in the wood lot," Julie argued. "He got Juan and went to check their fields."

Nodding, Aveline said, "They're keeping a close eye on the crop so they know the best moment to get the potatoes out of the ground."

"So let's go over to Lucas's farm and see him." She giggled. "And his goats! We've got time."

"We don't."

A strange look crossed the girl's face. "I've got to go home already? I just got here, and Daddy—"

"Whoa!" She put up her hands in fake surrender. She hoped the pose would keep the *kind* from guessing the truth. Her *daed*'s assistant, Neal, had called earlier to let the Lampels know the car would be a couple of hours late. Apparently, according to *Daed*, who'd taken the call in the barn, there was a meeting Philip couldn't get out of, and he'd asked if Julie could stay until he was able to collect her. *Daed* had agreed before passing along the message to Aveline. "You're not going home yet. I've got a surprise for you."

"A surprise? For me? What is it?"

"If I tell you, it won't be a surprise, ain't so?" Holding out her hand, she smiled when the girl put hers in it. "Here it comes."

Julie started to ask another question, then gasped when she saw the dozen youngsters romping toward them. When she noticed one of the kids pushing Daisy's chair, she squealed and ran to greet her friend.

Aveline welcomed the group of *kinder*. Other than Daisy, they ranged in age from seven to about thirteen. The perfect age for Julie. It had taken her most of the past two days, talking to people at the Kuhns' as well as at church, to arrange for the *kinder* to come today. Everyone had been enthusiastic to help as soon as she'd spoken of the lonely *Englisch kind*.

Motioning to the kids, Aveline said, "Julie, you've met Daisy, and the rest are our scholars."

"Scholars?" Julie's nose wrinkled. "Why do you call them that?"

"It's the name we give to *kinder* in school."

"Kind of a serious name, isn't it?"

Daisy's smile spread across the group when she said, "We're serious about school when we're there, but we're most serious about playing baseball."

The other kids cheered, lifting bats, balls and mitts. It took less than ten minutes to set up an impromptu baseball diamond in an empty field out beyond the main barn. The grass was already tamped down because Aveline's older brothers had enjoyed a pickup game with their friends last night.

Aveline stood to one side while the *kinder* picked teams. She was pleased the scholars were thoughtful enough to have Julie be among the first chosen. The girl did high fives with her teammates, which delighted them.

"Do I need a ticket for this important game?"

came a deep voice from behind Aveline as the two teams took their places to start.

A heated shiver rippled along her as Lucas's question caressed her ears. Hoping that warmth wasn't visible on her face, she turned to find him right behind her, resting his hand on a fence pole. His face was shadowed by the brim of his straw hat, but his tanned neck and forearms glistened with sweat from whatever hard work he'd been doing. Her eyes focused on his hand, which was broader than the top of the pole. His fingers were rough and nicked from his time in the fields and working with his animals, but she knew they could be as gentle as a *boppli*'s when he comforted a frightened *kind*. Everything about him was a contradiction. Tough and gentle, shallow along with hints of depths he let no one see, affability mixed with shadows of loneliness.

He was a puzzle she wanted to solve. Yet she'd be foolish to delve into his mysteries because she suspected there were many layers within the labyrinth of what he hid, each answer leading to more questions that would entice her further. A woman could get lost that way. She must resist because she already felt disconnected from the person she'd been in Ontario before everything in her life had gone topsy-turvy.

Realizing she hadn't answered him when

his smile wavered, Aveline hurried to say, "Of course not! Join us."

He sat when she did on a knoll that gave them an excellent view of the players. The crack of the ball off the bat and the shrieks of excitement as a player reached a base or was tagged out overwhelmed the sound of the bugs whirring in the thickening heat of the late afternoon.

"This was a great idea, Aveline," he said as he draped his arm over his drawn-up knee. "Julie looks like she's having a great time."

"It's the best way for her to meet our kids."

He glanced at the sky. "She won't have much time."

"She's staying a bit later tonight." She explained the call *Daed* had received in the barn.

"That's odd, ain't so?"

"I thought so, but then I remembered how often Julie laments about eating alone. Perhaps Philip wants to make sure they can have supper together."

"Perhaps."

Aveline heard the disquiet in his voice and felt it echo inside her, forcing her to admit her own reaction hadn't been any different from his. She'd tried to quiet those anxious rumbles when *Daed* had assured her that Neal had acted as if the call had been nothing out of the ordinary.

And it probably was. Julie had mentioned how her *daed*'s meetings often ran long.

She looked toward a row of trees separating the farm from the properties to the east and the north. Was someone—the mysterious man whom Julie believed was observing her—among them?

"I haven't seen anyone," Lucas said quietly. Was he watching her as surreptitiously as she'd watched him during church?

"You've been looking?"

"*Ja*. Ever since Julie mentioned seeing someone."

"Me, too."

He gave her a lopsided grin. "That doesn't surprise me. You promised Philip you'd keep an eye on his daughter, and you're not a person who goes back on her promises."

"How do you know that? You don't know me that well."

"I know you're kind, and you're focused on helping others without the least bit of fanfare. Family means everything to you. You chase after your wayward calf, not because she's a valuable animal but because you care about her like a hen with a single chick."

"Aveline!" called Daisy before she could respond.

Relieved by the interruption, Aveline came to her feet. "What is it?"

"It's my turn at bat. I can hit, but Boppi Lynn isn't *gut* at helping me go around the bases."

Lucas chuckled and started to rise, but Aveline motioned for him to stay where he was.

"I can help," she said as she trotted over to where the girl's wheelchair was a short distance from the rubber mat they were using for home plate. "You hit the ball, Daisy, and I'll push you to first base."

"Or second or third."

"All the way to home." Julie's enthusiasm widened Daisy's smile as she rolled her chair closer to home plate. The catcher handed her a bat.

Standing to one side and praying that a wild pitch didn't come her way, Aveline watched one ball then another fly past Daisy's bat. The teen didn't bother to swing because they were so far outside the catcher had to jump up and chase after them.

"Throw one I can hit," called Daisy.

The pitcher clamped his teeth hard before he wound up and threw the ball. Daisy swung her bat hard and the ball arched along the third base line.

Aveline leaped forward and grasped the handles on the wheelchair. Bending her head as if running into a strong headwind, she pushed Daisy and Boppi Lynn to first base. As a wheel bumped over it, she looked up. The ball was rolling farther away in the outfield.

"Hold on!" she shouted.

Daisy cheered as they went toward second base. When the front wheel bumped into the base, the girl ordered, "Go! Go now! Go now, Aveline! Go!"

Not wasting a moment to check where the ball was, Aveline ran. The chair tried to skitter around second base, but she straightened it. She pumped her legs as fast as she could when she heard the other team's members calling to each other.

The ball whirled past her right ear. She started to slow. She couldn't get Daisy to third base before the ball got there.

"Don't stop!" Daisy shrieked.

Aveline stared in disbelief as the ball sailed over the third baseman's mitt and sped away.

"Hold on!" Pausing to make sure one of the wheels touched the base, she jerked the chair up on two wheels to make the turn toward home. Shouts and cheers came from every direction as both teams urged their players on.

Lucas jumped to his feet and clapped his hands as the front right wheel of Daisy's chair bumped over home. Julie rushed forward and threw her arms around the older girl. Aveline patted Daisy's shoulder but fought to get her breath enough to speak.

"That was so cool!" Julie cried as everyone came to add their congratulations. "Can you teach me to do that, Daisy? I've never hit a home run."

"Me neither. Not till today!" Daisy's voice was as breathless as if she'd run the bases herself. "I can't wait to do it again."

"I can." Aveline leaned forward and put her hands on her knees.

"You two are a great team," Lucas said as he offered his arm to Aveline.

She took it while Daisy wheeled away, recounting every moment as if none of them had been there. "Next time, it's your turn to run the bases."

"Can't today," he said as he patted her hand on his arm. "I need to get home and finish my evening chores. I let them slide while I came over to see how Julie was doing."

"I'm glad you stopped by. Julie was wondering when she'd see you."

"Work has been busy with getting ready for the harvest."

"I know. That's what I told her. I said you've got to keep an eye on the hills to make sure you dig out the potatoes at the right time."

"'Striking while the iron is hot' is an old saying for a *gut* reason."

"It's different with making cheese. We're busy in the months after the calves are born, but we don't have such a short window as you potato farmers do to get the crop out of the ground and sold."

"Winters don't send announcements about when the temperatures will drop, and if there's a freeze, the whole crop can be ruined in the ground." He put his hand on the fence pole as he had before, an easy pose she didn't believe because his shoulders were taut. "I think we've got another week before we need to start digging. It looks as if Mark's fields are going to be first because of how the sun hits them."

"There are a lot of things you've got to learn to raise potatoes, ain't so?"

"No more than you need to raise water buffalo." He glanced at the field. "Moobeam hasn't been over to visit in the past few days."

"She seems more content with the others now. Or it may be we've finally figured out how to keep her from slipping out."

She savored his easygoing laugh. The tension that had strangled her since she'd overheard Mattie and Kirsten talking about her in the kitchen vanished. She dared to believe the misunderstandings were behind them, and she could count Lucas among her friends.

Something sharp pierced her. A denial to her own thoughts, so strong she knew friendship with him wouldn't be enough. She looked away so he couldn't see her face. She wished she hadn't, because her eyes locked on *Mamm*, who stood on the porch, watching her with Lucas.

Mamm was as stiff as a soldier on parade, a sure sign she was upset.

Mamm was growing more and more displeased about the time Aveline spent with Lucas, whom she now believed was unsuitable as a husband. At first, Aveline had thought *Mamm*'s change of heart was a ploy to make Lucas seem appealing, but she had to wonder if *Mamm* had other reasons for disliking him. Her *mamm* was perceptive when it came to others, a skill she'd employed while helping her sons find future spouses.

What had *Mamm* seen in Lucas that Aveline had missed?

Chapter Eleven

❧

As he walked away from the impromptu ball-field, Lucas listened to the kids enjoying their game and wished he could stay longer. Not to see the scholars play. Not to scan the tree line to make sure nobody was lurking there.

He wanted to spend time with Aveline. Doing so was foolish, and doing so could complicate his life. He'd seen Chalonna on the porch, her eyes narrowed as she'd watched him with her daughter. He hadn't been able to decipher her expression, but it hadn't been a smile. Was she calculating, as Aveline joined in the game, how to convince him to propose to her daughter?

Imagining Aveline as his bride, soft and warm in his arms, was easy to do. It was a *wunderbaar* thought but not a *wunderbaar* idea. He'd been led astray by such enticing thoughts in the past, and look where it'd gotten him. Alone and desperate

to prove he could get a woman—any woman—
to respond to his flirting. How could he know if
his burgeoning feelings for Aveline were real?

When he saw Aveline's *daed* in the barnyard,
he hesitated. Elam was checking his horse's hoof
by balancing its foreleg on his knee, and Lucas
didn't want to startle either man or horse when
they stood so close to each other.

Elam lowered the horse's leg and stood. Without
looking at Lucas, he said, "You've been around
here a lot."

Lucas recoiled, shocked by Elam's chilly comment. Didn't Aveline's *daed* realize Lucas was
trying to assist his daughter help Julie?

He started to explain, then realized Elam
wasn't listening. The man walked away, talking to the horse as he led the black gelding out
of the barn.

Elam Lampel was a man of few words. Everyone knew that, guessing he didn't often have a
chance to speak with his gabby wife. However,
Lucas had never imagined Elam would be rude
to him. He'd thought Elam was fair, willing to
let a man have a chance to explain.

Lucas stiffened as he recalled how Elam hadn't
wanted Lucas to take part in the discussions
about what to do with Philip's reward. Did Elam
think Lucas was too frivolous and useless? Inno-
cent flirting shouldn't stain a man's reputation.

But it had.

A motion caught his eye, and he saw Chalonna still standing on the porch. She'd crossed her arms over her chest. Her glare was unmistakable. She wanted him gone.

He headed to his buggy he'd left in the lane. Not greeting Aveline's *mamm* seemed odd, but he kept going in silence. Anything he said might get him one of her infamous tongue-lashings. It seemed Robin had been wrong when she'd said he wasn't any fun. He was at the center of a jest, and the joke was on him because the woman who was so super eager for her daughter to wed that she'd approached many of the single men in the community had dismissed him as unworthy of her daughter.

The irony of it weighed on him as if he carried Moobeam on his shoulders. He got in his buggy and drove away, dragging his wounded pride behind him.

Julie jumped out of the car three days later, as excited to be there as she was every day. Clearly, visiting the plain community was an endless adventure of discovery for her. "Aveline," she called, "let's go and see Lucas's goats today."

"We did that last week." Aveline stepped back to let the *kind* into the house. She pretended not to notice *Mamm*'s frown. It was *Mamm*'s constant expression when Julie was there.

Maybe Aveline should go to Juan's house. She didn't want Julie upset by *Mamm*'s glowers. On the other hand, she didn't want to expose the girl to the virus that had kept Evie and her great-*grossmammi* in bed for the past two days.

"I know," Julie said, "but let's go. C'mon, Aveline. You like going to see Lucas and his goats. You always have a big smile while we're there. You know you do."

With a "tsk," *Mamm* walked out of the kitchen, closing the door between it and the front room with a resounding slam. The theatrics were wasted because Julie paid no attention. She was intent only on seeing the goats.

Aveline managed a smile because she didn't want the girl to become aware of the strain left in *Mamm*'s wake. The mention of Lucas's name vexed *Mamm*. Had he said something to *Mamm* to annoy her? Aveline had tried to talk to her *daed* about it, but he'd changed the subject before she could say anything. She would have discussed it with Lucas, but she hadn't seen him since he'd left after Daisy's home run. He and his brother and cousin were busy with getting their equipment and horses ready for harvesting the potatoes.

She missed talking with him. She missed seeing how much he cared for Julie and her safety. She missed...him.

That was the truth she couldn't deny. She'd looked forward to seeing Lucas. Without him, there was a big void in her days.

Handing Julie an apron, she said, "Let's get to work. I've got to get these loaves of raisin bread baked if we're going to send a couple home to your *daed*."

The girl froze, her face growing hard. "He won't be home tonight to eat it. He and Neal flew to Toronto early this morning, and they won't be home until tomorrow."

"They've been traveling a lot, ain't so?"

"*Ja*." Her tone was so inconsolable, Aveline didn't feel like grinning at her easy use of *Deitsch*.

"You miss your *daed*." She reached out for the *kind*.

Julie wrapped her arms around Aveline's waist. "I do."

"I'm sure Neal's family miss him."

She shook her head so hard her braids slapped her shoulders. "Neal's divorced, and he doesn't see his kids much. He complains about it. A lot."

"That's sad."

She stuffed her hands into the pockets of her jeans. "Not having a wife makes it easy for him to go, and Daddy is a widower. They can travel because their wives don't insist they're home in time to sit at the supper table with their families." Her mouth straightened into a tight line. "Not that it makes any difference for Neal. Since the divorce, his wife and kids haven't had anything to do with him."

"How do you know that?"

"I've heard him and Daddy talk. Neal gets really sad when he mentions his family. I know he fought to keep the divorce from happening, but it didn't do him any good." She picked up one of the chocolate-chip cookies Aveline had baked earlier and popped it into her mouth. "He's sad and mad and in a bad mood."

"Then maybe it's a *gut* thing he's traveling, ain't so?"

Julie selected a flour-dusted raisin that had fallen out of the dough and rolled it between her thumb and forefinger as she pondered Aveline's words. "I wish Daddy didn't have to go with him." Her nose wrinkled. "I hate eating by myself. I tried putting Cuddles in one of the chairs, but it didn't help."

"Your stuffed bear isn't great at keeping a conversation going, ain't so?" She waited for the girl's reaction.

When Julie sighed, the joy she'd showed during her previous visits gone, Aveline wanted to give the girl another hug and tell her everything would get better. She couldn't make such a promise. Philip must do that.

Did he realize how much his trips were hurting his daughter? Aveline couldn't believe he did. Everything she'd seen about him suggested he was a *gut* man and a *gut daed*.

So what had changed?

As she looked at the *kind*, she knew what had changed at the DeSares' house wasn't as important as Julie's reaction. She must find a solution, something to make the girl feel less alone.

Aveline considered the problem the rest of the day. Each time she thought she had a solution, she discarded it and started over. When she finally found an idea she believed might work, she knew she couldn't do it on her own. Nor could Lucas help her, because he was a bachelor. However, his brother was married, and Julie adored Evie. Maybe…just maybe…it would work.

First she needed to share her idea with Juan and Annalise. She tried to slip out right after Julie left to go home, but she wasn't quick enough. Aveline's ears still rang when she walked to the Kuepfers' door. *Mamm* had been shrill as she told Aveline the *Englisch kind* needed to find other places to spend her days. Why hadn't Aveline listened when *Mamm* told her getting mixed up with *Englischers* would keep her from her most important task—finding a husband?

"If you take care of someone else's *kind*, how will you have a chance to meet a man who will give you *kinder* of your own?" *Mamm* had knocked around the pans in the sink, creating a din in the kitchen.

"It's only for a couple of weeks until school starts." Aveline had thought that was a reasonable argument.

Not *Mamm*. The noise from the sink had gotten louder, and Aveline had to fight her instinct to put her hands over her ears. The reprimand would have become more strident if she did that. *Mamm* had wanted to make sure she heard every word.

Daed and her brothers entering the kitchen had ended the diatribe. Her brothers had scooted out, not wanting *Mamm*'s caustic words aimed at them. Aveline had slipped away with her brothers. When they'd asked her what was going on and she'd explained, she was astonished when they took *Mamm*'s side. Aveline should be focused on finding a husband.

Throwing up her hands, she'd left to stride along the road lit by the long, lazy summer twilight. Why couldn't her family see that helping one *kind* was the best way to show any interested men she was compassionate and loving?

"Ugh," she muttered as she turned down the lane to Juan's house. "Now they've got me thinking marriage is the most important thing in my life." She grimaced, but forced a smile when she rapped on the door then opened it. "Anyone here?"

"Aveline," said Annalise with a smile, "how *wunderbaar* to see you. We're just about to have cake and lemonade. Will you join us?"

She nodded. "*Danki.* I'm sorry to be bothering you so late."

Grossmammi Fern motioned for Aveline to sit across the table from her and next to Evie. The two were flanked by the dogs, as always.

"How are you feeling?" Aveline asked as she took off her black bonnet and hung it next to Juan's straw hat.

"Fit as I've ever been," the old woman said with a grin. "No germ is going to keep me down long."

"I'm fits, too," Evie chimed in.

Aveline smiled. "I'm glad to hear that."

"Sit down and join us," Annalise said from where she stood by the counter.

"*Ja,*" *Grossmammi* Fern added, "we're enjoying the slow sunset. We won't have them much longer. Winter's coming."

"Not before we get the crops in, I hope," said Juan from his seat at the head of the table. He smiled at his wife when she put a brimming glass of freshly squeezed lemonade and a large piece of cake in front of him. "I don't think I'd mind the short days as much if they weren't so cold."

"Long days betters in summer," Evie pronounced as Annalise served her. The girl unerringly reached for the spoon her *mamm* held.

Amazement and gratitude swirled through Aveline. Though God had made Evie blind, He had given her intelligence. The little girl might get stumped the first time she encountered something new, but by the next time she faced that challenge, she'd found a way to overcome it.

"I came to ask a favor," Aveline said.

"What can we do to help?" asked Juan.

"Would you consider inviting Julie DeSare to stay here with you when her *daed* has to be away on business? She's lonely, and the girls adore each other. We could ask Daisy to help. In many ways, she isn't any older than Julie."

"Fern will be here, too." Juan smiled at the tiny woman who was savoring her cake.

"I will be," the older woman said. "I like that young *Englisch* girl. She has nice manners, and she's willing to try something new." She chuckled. "Like chow-chow."

Annalise looked at her husband. "This may be the solution we've been looking for. Having Evie and the dogs on the construction site is asking for trouble. If Daisy came over, she could keep an eye on the two girls and the dogs."

"Daisy and Evie have already found plenty of mischief together," Juan said, his face stern as he turned to his wife. "Are you sure about this?"

"I am."

Juan picked up his fork. "It's chaotic with us getting ready to move but—"

"The mores, the merriers," Evie said around a mouthful of cake.

Juan chuckled. "You're right, Evie. *Ja*, Daisy and Evie got into mischief, but they never did anything to endanger themselves or anyone else."

"Julie is too grown up," Aveline said. "With Evie and Daisy, she can be a youngster."

Annalise put her hand over her husband's. "So you agree, Juan?"

"I think it's a *wunderbaar* idea. Let's give them something to do like teaching Julie *Deitsch*."

"How about the harmonica?" asked his wife with a smile. "Evie has been playing one every chance she can since you taught her, Juan. I'm sure she'd love to teach the others."

"Daisy isn't interested, but Julie may be," he said.

"In return, Julie can teach the girls recipes she's learned from her *daed*'s cook. She has wild ideas about what should go in a tortilla."

Evie grinned. "Loves tacos and quesadillas."

"*Gut*." Downing the last of her lemonade, Aveline glanced around the table. These people had been casual neighbors just weeks ago. Now they were dear friends who'd banded together to help a *kind*.

"I assume," Juan said, breaking into her thoughts, "you need to discuss this with Julie's *daed*."

"*Ja*."

"Do you want Lucas involved in that discussion? I'm heading over there, so I can ask him. If he can't, I'll let you know."

A frisson of anticipation swirled through her but she had to say, "I'll be glad to have him along if he's not busy."

"I'm sure he can spare an hour or two for you."

"I hope so." She was sure her face was ablaze. Somehow, she got to her feet, thanked them for their hospitality, and rushed out the door.

She had to have her blush under control before she got home. If *Mamm* saw it and realized Aveline was thinking of Lucas, the uproar would be worse. Instead, Aveline needed to focus on helping Julie. It might be the sole way to continue ignoring the supplications of her obstinate heart.

Lucas shouldn't have been amazed at how quickly the familiar black car arrived at his farm two mornings later just before breakfast time. When Juan had stopped in a couple nights previous and shared the idea Aveline had presented, Lucas had agreed. It was an excellent solution to help the girl feel less alone.

When he'd left a message on Philip's cell phone after Juan let him know Aveline wanted a meeting with Julie's *daed*, he'd gotten one in return the next day at the phone shack. Philip had time to meet with him and Aveline first thing the following morning. The message included an apology that the hour had to be so early, but he was flying to Edmonton after lunch.

With barely enough time to change out of his work clothes covered with hay and grime from milking, Lucas was glad the car had stopped at the Lampels' farm first. Otherwise, he wouldn't have been ready.

He greeted Randall, who handed him a cup of *kaffi* as he slid into the back seat, and then turned to do the same to Aveline. His words faded, unspoken, when he discovered how close her face was to his. He'd gone farther into the seat than he'd planned, and he was encroaching on her side of the car. Knowing he should back away, he couldn't move for a long, very pleasant moment as his lips were a hand's breadth from hers.

But sense prevailed, and Lucas shifted away. She lowered her luminous eyes that invited him to move closer. Randall tried to keep a casual conversation going on the way to the DeSares' house. Aveline didn't say much, sipping her *kaffi* as if her life depended on each swallow. Wanting to ask her what was wrong, he was certain she wasn't worried about the upcoming meeting with Philip. Was she upset because his farm had kept him so busy he hadn't had a chance to stop by and see how Julie was doing?

He hid his grimace behind his own cup of *kaffi*. Going to her place would have meant speaking with her parents, and they'd made it crystal clear they'd prefer he didn't visit. Though he wasn't surprised by Chalonna, he'd thought Elam would remain welcoming. Something had soured Aveline's *daed* to him. He had no idea what it might have been.

Did Aveline know? He opened his mouth to ask her, then clamped it shut. He didn't need to add to the misery displayed on her face. Because of him or something else? Another question he'd be unwise to ask.

Randall's attempts to keep the conversation going failed before they were halfway across the Island. They rode the rest of the way in silence.

It wasn't any better when they reached the house. The eastern-facing windows glistened in the sunlight, so bright he had to look away. Spots remained in front of his eyes as he followed Aveline to the front door.

He could see well enough to discover Philip's assistant was in the foyer. Even if he'd been blinded by the sunshine, he would have recognized the cool, detached tone belonging to Neal Mathers.

"Philip is busy," the *Englischer* announced as if speaking a royal decree.

Aveline's voice was velvet-covered steel. "We know he's busy, so we don't want to keep him waiting."

He thought Neal would insist on them leaving and returning another day. Footsteps sounded behind the other man, and Lucas looked past him to see a maid carrying towels into one of the house's many bathrooms.

Lucas took Neal's distraction to ask, "Do you know where Philip is? Like Aveline said, we don't want to delay your trip."

"I'm right here," Philip said, coming forward as he finished arranging his tie. "Neal, get yourself breakfast. I won't be long."

Lucas thought Neal would protest, but the man nodded and disappeared in the direction of the kitchen.

Philip led the way into a small, cozy room off to one side of the grand living room. It had soft furniture facing a large television. The television was on, with words crawling in several lines at the bottom of the screen, but it was silent. Sitting with his back to it, Lucas waited as Philip offered them more *kaffi* and a breakfast pastry.

Aveline didn't take any. Instead, she jumped right in. "Philip, we wanted to talk to you because Julie let me know she's unhappy with how much you've been traveling."

He sighed, his face grim. "I hate it. I'd intended to stay close to home the whole summer, but Neal insists I need to join him to see concerns he has in the manufacturing facilities."

Though he wondered what Philip DeSare's company made, Lucas didn't allow his curiosity to tease him to ask. Rodney must know, so Lucas would ask the bishop later. For now, he should keep his mind on the problem at hand.

"We understand the demands of owning a business," Lucas said. "A farmer faces many of the same ones, though on a much smaller scale."

"A problem when it's your problem is never small."

"*Ja.*" He appreciated how the *Englischer*'s words suggested their business responsibilities were equal. In a way, they were, because if Lucas's harvest failed, he'd face bankruptcy as Philip would if his company ran into bad times. "While Aveline and I understand, Julie doesn't."

"I've tried to explain to her, and she tells me she gets it." He tapped his fingers on his chin, a sign, Lucas had come to learn, he was upset.

"She knows my work is important to all my employees."

"As long as she doesn't think your work is the most important thing to you."

Philip's brows rose almost to his hair. "She should know that's not true, Lucas. She's the most important thing in the world to me."

Aveline said, "That's why we're here to offer a temporary solution."

He leaned forward as he did each time he believed a consensus was about to be reached. "Tell me."

"School will be starting soon, and that should help ease Julie's loneliness."

"I've been making plans to assure that."

"*Gut*," Lucas said. "There are at least two weeks before school begins, and that's why we wanted to talk with you. I'm sure Julie's told you a lot about my brother's family."

"Is that Evie's family?"

"*Ja.*"

Philip's smile returned. "Julie adores Evie and her dogs. Is Daisy another member of the family?"

"Daisy is our cousin," Lucas replied.

"She talks about the two girls and draws pictures of them playing together. I'm sorry I haven't been able to have Evie and Daisy visit here. My work schedule…" His smile wavered. "I didn't expect Neal would need so much guidance at this point. He's always been able to handle things on his own. His divorce changed him. A lot." Squaring his shoulders, he said, "Tell me what you've come up with."

Lucas listened while Aveline presented their idea of the *kind* staying with his brother's family, including overnight. Not once did she suggest pity was the reason. Instead she spoke of how the *kinder* would like to have Julie join them in their games in the last remaining days before school began. When she spoke of how, as a *kind*, she'd been so eager for summer vacation and within weeks had been as keen to return to school because the days without the structure of school had begun to drag.

"I was the same," Philip said. "Counting down the days until we were out of class and then counting down the time until I could go back. I'd forgotten that. I'm not sure what to say about your offer."

"We're hoping you'd agree," she replied.

"You've already done so much for her. So much for both of us." His mouth edged into a straight line. "You won't let me do anything for you. Your bishop wants to talk to me about that blasted reward. I don't understand why I can't help you as you're trying to help us."

"You're talking about money, Philip," Lucas

said. "We're talking about a *kind* who's lonely when you're traveling. There's a big difference."

Philip tapped his chin again with his forefinger and then sent a servant to bring his daughter to the office.

Julie arrived less than a minute later, rubbing sleep out of her eyes, which grew large when she saw Lucas and Aveline.

"What's going on?" the girl asked. "Are you not going away, Daddy?"

Philip took her hands and folded them in his much larger ones. "I have to go on this trip, but while I'm away, would you like to stay with Lucas's brother's family?"

"With Evie?" Her eyes brightened. "Yes. Yes! Yes! I want to stay with her. That way I get to see her dogs and the animals." She gave them a cock-eyed grin. "And I'll see you, Aveline and Lucas."

"Nice save," Philip said with a chuckle.

His daughter wrinkled her nose at him before breaking into laughter of her own. Irrepressible, she turned to Aveline. "Will we see Daisy and Boppi Lynn? Can we play baseball? Will you show me how to hit a home run?"

"*Ja. Ja.* I would if I knew how." Aveline stroked the girl's hair. "Let's take each day as it dawns and enjoy each day God has given us."

Philip took a surreptitious glance at his watch before saying, "Go and pack, Julie. I'll check in a minute to make sure you've got everything you need."

"Okay." She whirled to leave, then stopped as abruptly as if she'd run into an invisible wall. Spinning, she flung her arms around her *daed.* "Thanks, Daddy! I'm going to miss you though I'm with Evie and Daisy and Boppi Lynn."

"I know." He kissed her cheek. "I'll miss you though I'm with Neal and lawyers and the board of directors."

Her nose scrunched. "Poor Daddy."

"Yes. Poor me." He turned her around and gave her a gentle push toward the stairs. "Go and pack."

As the *kind*'s footfalls faded up the stairs, Philip's smile disappeared. "I hate leaving her so long."

"She hates to have you gone so long," Aveline said, "but the time will pass quickly because she'll be playing with other *kinder.*"

"Much faster for her than for me." A faint smile returned to his lips but his eyes remained somber. "While Julie is upstairs, there is something I need to discuss with you. I don't know how you handle money in your community."

Aveline straightened. "Philip, the reward is in Rodney's hands."

"I understand that. Your bishop and I are planning to sit down together when I return from this trip. I think we'll be able to hammer something out that will satisfy everyone."

Lucas wished he could agree with Philip, but he'd seen enough of the *Englischer* to learn the head of DeSare Industries expected to get his way in any negotiation. Philip hadn't dealt with Rodney Wolfe, so he might be in for a big surprise.

"However," Philip went on, "I insist on giving your brother's family money for Julie's room and board."

Lucas was about to argue that one girl didn't eat much when Aveline said, "We'll talk to Juan. I'm sure you'll be able to work out an arrangement to satisfy both of you."

Why would she say something like that? There were plenty of vegetables ripening in the garden. In fact, Julie would be doing *them* a favor by helping them eat the generous harvest.

Lucas kept his question silent until they emerged from the house. The car wasn't waiting for them, so he took advantage of nobody else nearby to ask her.

"We need to give him the sense he's contributing something," Aveline said.

"You know that's not necessary. We're implored to watch out for—"

"If you quote me the verse about taking care of widows and *kinder*, I'll clap my hand over your mouth."

I'd prefer you put your lips over my mouth. He couldn't say that aloud because it would tear away the last of his self-control. He would grasp her by the shoulders and pull her into his arms. With her lips against his, he would tell her the things he hadn't been able to put in words. About how he was eager for every chance to meet. About how he thought of her when she wasn't there. About how he'd wanted to kiss her for what seemed like forever.

He remained silent as the car came around a corner of the house and slowed for them to get in. Another opportunity lost, but how had he lost something that never had been or—if her parents had their way—never would be his?

Chapter Twelve

"Do you want to know what I've heard?" Julie asked as she prowled around the Lampels' kitchen the following week. She'd spent every other day with Evie and her family but Aveline had invited the girl over to give the Kuepfers a break. Not that they'd asked for one, but she worried Juan was overtired. She doubted he had much time to rest with two active girls and two rambunctious dogs in his house. She didn't want fatigue to retard his progress in regaining his eyesight.

Besides, Aveline had the house to herself. *Mamm* and *Daed* had driven into Montague to enjoy a walk around the harbor and a chance to have a nice lunch at one of the nearby restaurants. Had *Mamm* or Aveline been more surprised when *Daed* suggested an excursion in the middle of the week? Aveline had seen the twinkle in his eyes. She took it as his silent permission to let Julie visit without coming face-to-face with *Mamm*.

Aveline was amazed that *Mamm* had accepted her assertion Lucas would never be more to her than a neighbor. Though she shouldn't have been surprised. *Mamm* hadn't made any secret of her belief that Lucas would string Aveline along, never offering marriage.

Was *Mamm* right about that? Aveline would have been happy about that a few weeks ago, but something had shifted in her heart since she'd dared to believe he'd wanted to kiss her after they'd talked to Philip about Julie staying with Evie and her family. The expression in Lucas's eyes had been so warm, so inviting, so...everything.

"Aveline?" came Julie's impatient voice, and Aveline had to wonder how long she'd been lost in thought. "Don't you want to know what I heard?"

"Remember repeating hearsay can bring dismay," Aveline said as she mixed dough for the three apple pies she wanted to have ready for supper. Once she filled the pans, she'd put the pies into the oven and turn on the ceiling fan that ran on compressed air from the diesel engine in the building next to the big barn.

"It isn't a rumor." Julie halted, tapped her finger on her chin in a copy of her *daed*'s thoughtful motion. "Evie told me, and she should know because it's happening on her farm."

She dribbled another spoon of icy water into the dough. "Are you talking about the plans to move her *mamm*'s woodworking shop before they begin looking for a buyer for the farm?"

"You know about that?" Julie asked.

"*Ja.* I've known about it for a while. Lucas and Annalise don't need two farms. Once the construction is completed on Lucas's house to make it big enough for all of them, they plan to move there. Annalise will need her woodworking shop, and it's easier to move it than build a new one."

"Why didn't you tell me?" the girl demanded.

Aveline put the ball of dough on the table and reached for her rolling pin. "I wasn't sure if you'd be interested."

"You didn't think I'd be interested?" Julie's voice rose on every word. "Evie says they're going to carry the barn to Lucas's farm."

She shook her head. "Just next door to Juan's farm."

"A whole building?" Julie scowled. "You're kidding me, aren't you?"

"No. *Komm* here." She held out the rolling pin to the *kind.* "Let me show you how to roll out the crust and put it in the pan."

Julie took the tool but her attention wasn't on

the task. "They can't *carry* a building that far. It's impossible."

Aveline smiled as she guided in rolling out the pie dough. "Slow. Smooth. Gentle." As Julie followed her instructions, she added, "They'll have lots of help. For a building of that size, they'll need about fifty volunteers."

"Who would volunteer to *carry* a building?"

"I would," came a voice from the other side of the kitchen.

Julie's head snapped up a second before Aveline's. Dropping the rolling pin on the dough, the girl exclaimed, "Lucas! I didn't think you were coming over here today."

"I didn't either," he said as he set his straw hat on an empty peg by the door.

Wiping flour off her hands and onto a hand towel, Aveline asked, "So what brings you here?"

"I discovered you were missing something."

"Oh, no! Did Moobeam get out? I thought we'd had the fence fixed so she couldn't slip out."

"Not you. Julie." He smiled as he held out his hand. "Is this yours?"

The girl squealed with delight as she took a hair clip from Lucas and began to twirl in her excitement.

Lucas's grin widened when his gaze met Aveline's. How could she have thought he was a man of no substance? He was happy he could bring happiness to a *kind* who hungered for it.

Putting the towel on the table next to the dough, Aveline wondered how Philip could dote on his daughter and not understand Julie needed his attention. Lucas seemed to know how to make the girl happy.

As he does you. She stiffened at the unexpected thought before asking why it was unexpected. Her opinions of flippant, too-smoothly-charming Lucas Kuepfer had changed since the day they'd found Julie in the woods.

As if Aveline had said the *kind*'s name aloud, Julie stopped. She bounced the clip into the air. "Daddy gave me this, and I didn't know where it was."

"It was in the goats' pen." He tapped the clip. "If I remember, it had a couple of silk flowers on it. The goats must have considered those quite a treat."

Aveline smiled when Julie giggled. The *kind* adored the goats so much, she would have let them nibble at everything she owned.

"Go and see if it still works," Aveline said, motioning toward the bathroom.

"Check it's clean," the girl said with a grin.

"I made sure there wasn't any goat slobber on it," Lucas replied, earning a peal of laughter from Julie.

The girl skipped out of the kitchen and Aveline became aware of how otherwise alone she and Lucas were. That seldom happened. It was unnerving. She gripped the rolling pin and began moving it over the pastry.

"What horrible thing did that dough do to you?" Lucas chuckled. "You're beating it like it's a rug."

She arranged the pie crust in the pan and sought something to say. Something other than telling him how much she wanted him to kiss her. No, she mustn't be a *dummkopf*. Days ago, she'd been distressed because he hadn't flirted with her as he did with other women. Now she was distressed because he had…and she'd been foolish enough to believe he'd been sincere.

"Aveline?" A hint of sorrow clung to his voice, and she guessed he was confused why she hadn't laughed, too.

"Sorry. Lost in thought." That much was the truth, but she could have said she felt completely lost.

"You know what I've been thinking?"

"What?"

He grinned. "We haven't had our *gut* friends stalking us every time we stepped out of the house."

With a gasp, she said, "You mean the reporters."

"They seem to have given up."

"At long last!" She spooned the bowl of apples she'd already sliced and mixed with flour, spices and butter into the last pie pan. She topped them with the brown sugar mix she'd prepared earlier.

"I kind of miss have them hanging around."

She looked up, hoping to see his eyes twinkling. Instead they were dim with anxiety. "Why do you want them here, Lucas?"

"Having extra eyes around means if someone is…" He lowered his voice as he stepped closer until his voice brushed her cheek like a caress. She wanted to melt into the warmth, but his next words froze her to her center as he switched to *Deitsch* so when Julie returned, she couldn't understand what he said. "If someone is watching her as she believes, I don't think they'd be bold enough to try something with others around."

"I never considered that." She shifted her gaze to the open bathroom door where the soft lift of Julie's singing drifted toward them. "She wants to watch the building being moved tomorrow morning. I'll make sure there are plenty of friendly eyes on her. After all, you know *Mamm* never misses anything." She tried to make it a joke but it fell flat. She carried two pies to the stove and reached to open the oven door with her elbow.

"Let me." He lowered the door and held it in place.

As the oven's heat swarmed out, Aveline put the pies in with care before turning to get the last one. She set it beside the others and stepped aside as he closed the door. "Lucas, tomorrow morning I will try to keep her beside me."

"*Mariyefrieh?*" asked Julie from behind them. "That means tomorrow morning, doesn't it? Are you talking about moving the building to Juan's farm?"

Exchanging a glance with Lucas, Aveline realized an intelligent girl like Julie must have already learned some *Deitsch* words and phrases. They couldn't use the language any longer and assume she wouldn't comprehend.

The rattle of buggy wheels on the drive kept Aveline from answering. She glanced toward the door. *Mamm* usually wasn't rude to someone's face, but *Mamm* didn't want Lucas or Julie there.

"Let's go," Lucas said, holding out his hand to Julie. "We can escape out the front."

Julie paused. "Will you be there tomorrow, Aveline?"

"*Ja.*"

"Great! Let's hang out together."

Aveline nodded, then looked toward the door.

Lucas grasped her arm and squeezed it. "Don't worry. We'll be gone before anyone knows we were here."

"Wait!" she called as he led the girl into the

front room. She snatched his hat off the peg, then ran into the living room to hand it to him.

He gave her a smile and quick wink. "*Danki* for protecting me, Aveline."

"Both of us." Julie grinned before scurrying out the door Lucas opened.

"See you *mariyefrieh*," he said as he followed the *kind*.

"*Ja*, tomorrow morning," Aveline breathed as she shut the door and rushed into the kitchen before the rear door opened.

Mamm blustered in, complaining about the crowds along the river in Montague and the long line at the ladies' room by the tourist information center. She wasn't happy about the amount of traffic and how long they'd had to wait at one stop sign.

There might have been other grievances aired, but Aveline had stopped listening to anything but the happy beat of her heart as she thought about seeing Lucas the next day. She was being foolish, but she was going to enjoy every moment of the happiness while she could.

The morning of the move dawned steamy and without a cloud in the sky. Buckets of water and ladles had been gathered by the tables where, half an hour ago, mountains of scrambled eggs and bacon had been arranged next to platters of bread, white and cornbread, as well as biscuits. Large bowls had steamed with sausage gravy, while the women had been kept busy chasing away dogs and kids who wanted to help themselves to glistening sausages. The platters and bowls were now empty, and donuts were no longer piled high like white snowbanks.

Lucas wiped his fingers on a napkin and tossed it into a trash can at one end of the table. He scanned the crowd gathered in Annalise's backyard. More than sixty men were congregating next to the small barn that would be moved to Juan's farm.

It had already been emptied, and the heavy woodworking machinery moved down the road. The building, lifted off its foundation, had been set on a series of two-by-fours beneath the floor joists.

As he went to join them, greeting his neighbors—both plain and *Englisch*—Lucas looked back at the food tables. Aveline stood there with her arm around Julie's shoulders. The girl's smile was broad, like Evie's and Daisy's. The three girls, along with Aveline, had stuck together through breakfast as if they were sewn pieces in a quilt.

His gaze caught Aveline's. When she gave the slightest nod, he returned it before hurrying to climb into the shop.

The floor had been pulled off, the boards already at Juan's farm where they'd be reinstalled once the barn was in its new location. Braces kept the walls and roof from collapsing. Doors had been removed, but the windows remained in place.

Stepping between two floor joists at the rear, Lucas greeted the men around him. Some he recognized. Others he didn't, so he guessed they were from one of the other districts on the Island. When his young cousin, Daryn, stepped into the space in front of him, he saw excitement in the teen's eyes. Daryn stuck his straw hat in a space along the walls, and Lucas pushed his own in next to it. He didn't want his hat falling off and getting trampled.

"Room for us?" called an *Englisch* voice, and he saw Philip DeSare and his assistant Neal Mathers clambering inside. Philip was smiling, but Neal's expression announced he'd rather be anywhere else.

Philip found a place next to Lucas, but his assistant volunteered to be outside the building to help guide it into place on its arrival. With a big grin, Philip said, "Well, this is a first for me. Moving a building by carrying it."

"Did you get something to eat?" Lucas asked. "You want to be fortified for this, especially on a hot, humid morning."

"I'll do my best to keep up."

"There are other jobs that—"

The *Englischer* became serious. "Let me help with this one thing to repay your brother and his wife."

Lucas gave the other man a quick pat on the shoulder, then looked toward the front of the building where Elam Lampel jumped onto a floor joist by the open door and gave a shout of, "Ready!"

Bending, Lucas wrapped his hands around the hard edges of the board in front of him. Elam called for them to start, and Lucas lifted. He heard Philip grunt as he did the same. With slow, shuffling steps, but moving in precision as one, the men moved the building forward. It wasn't quiet inside. A few of the men kept talking, and Elam would bellow for the front of the building or the rear to move to the right or left.

Elam called a stop when the building reached the main road. Lucas lowered the joist he held along with three other men to let the small barn balance on the ground. He took a deep breath and looked around at the already sweat-drenched volunteers. Men and teenagers were packed like sardines in the barn.

Out on the road, Benjamin was holding back the curious crowd that had gathered. He'd also been given the job of stopping traffic while the barn was carried along the two-lane road. Through one of the windows, Lucas could see Mattie's husband discussing with Elam the next part of the journey. They'd carried it about fifty meters and had about three times that distance to go.

"How are you doing, Philip?" he asked.

"Like I'm getting the most intense cardio workout of my life."

Leaning forward, Lucas grinned at his cousin. "You doing okay, Daryn?"

"When I was a kid," the boy said between pants, "I wanted to be part of what looked like a millipede with a barn on its back. Now…not so sure." He chuckled.

"It's satisfying work."

"Tell that to my hands." His palms were imprinted with the pattern of the woodgrain from the joist he'd been carrying.

Lucas chuckled and raised his own. "I'm considering it the sign of a job well done."

"Not yet."

Daryn's grim tone made Lucas laugh. "Don't you think those ropes you'll be using when you work a herd out west are going to leave marks on your hands?"

"I guess so." His smile became genuine as it did each time someone mentioned his dream of being a cowboy.

Philip smiled. "You want to work on a ranch?"

"*Ja*," Daryn said. "Some day."

"I know a guy who's always looking for men who aren't afraid of hard work. Let's talk after we get this barn moved."

Daryn's eager smile made him look no older than Daisy. "I'd like that, sir."

"No sirs between men who are working on the same team. Call me Philip."

The teen's chest puffed out as he nodded, but he didn't get a chance to reply because Elam called for everyone to turn to their left while they carried the barn along the road. It was simpler to turn the volunteers than the building.

By the time the shop was propped on the footers not far from Juan's equipment storage shed, sweat had drenched Lucas's shirt. The others around him were soaked, as well, but everyone looked satisfied.

Food was waiting by Juan's house. As if they hadn't eaten less than an hour before, the men fell on the food like a ravenous horde. *Kaffi* and other drinks were swallowed in a single gulp.

When Lucas walked with Philip toward where the *kinder* had gathered on the porch, the *Englischer* halted and asked, "Where are they?"

Lucas didn't need to ask about whom Philip was talking. A quick glance at the women and youngsters revealed that, though Daisy and Evie were sitting side by side while Daisy and other girls were sewing, neither Aveline nor Julie was there.

"I don't know," Lucas said.

"If something happened—"

"Too many people around," he interrupted, though he knew everyone's attention had been on the barn, not on a young *Englisch* girl. "Let me check inside."

Before he could move, Aveline emerged from the door with Julie by her side. When Julie sat beside Daisy's wheelchair, he heard Julie say, "I don't know how to sew."

"So we'll start you with stuffing then," the ever-practical Daisy said.

Aveline selected two flaps of brown fuzzy fabric. "What do you think this is, Julie?"

"It looks like roadkill." Julie made a face.

The *kinder* laughed, and the girl relaxed. Beside him, Lucas sensed Philip's tension falling away, too.

"Use your imagination," Aveline urged. "What do you think it'll be when it's finished?"

Julie took the fabric and turned it over. Her eyes widened when she touched a pair of cloth horns on the head. "It's a goat!"

"It will be a toy when you stuff it with scraps of fabric and foam. When it's nice and plump, I'll sew it closed."

One of the girls held out a bag. "Here's the stuffing."

"Thank you." Julie paused. "*Danki.*"

That brought smiles, and she ducked her head as she stuck her hand deep into the bag.

"Who's getting these toys?" Philip asked as he walked to the porch with Lucas.

"They're donated to the Mennonite Disaster Service," Aveline answered. "Have you heard of them? When there are big floods or fires or storms, they help people rebuild their homes and their lives. They're like second responders who come in before the first responders have left. They stay for as long as necessary to rebuild those lives and the community." She pulled another stuffed toy out of the big bag among the *kinder*. It was a horse. "A family may lose everything, even the *kinder*'s toys. This little toy can help a broken heart heal."

"It's a wonderful thing for you to do." Philip took a cup from one of the women handing them out to the volunteers. "That project and moving the barn. I admire how you are such a strong community."

"As Jesus told us," Aveline said as she smiled at Julie and the other *kinder*, "in the Book of John. 'This is my commandment, That ye love one another, as I have loved you.' He didn't say we should love just people we know and like, but everyone."

"Even Trace?" Julie asked, and Lucas heard Philip choke on his *kaffi* as his daughter spoke her kidnapper's name.

Aveline answered. "We believe in order to be forgiven, something we all need to do, we must forgive. God asks that of us."

"Where was God when that horrible man took me?"

Lucas felt Philip tremble beside him. The man had suffered almost as much as his *kind*, and no matter how Philip tried to conceal his true feelings by throwing himself into his work, he remained snared in anguish. The man's expression begged to be freed from the invisible jail he couldn't escape.

"God was with you. He never left you." Aveline folded the *kind*'s hands in hers, but her gaze moved toward the men. Her words were for them—and for herself—as much as for the girl. "He was there to give you strength, and then He sent Lucas and me to find you. What a *wunderbaar* gift He gave us, because now we're friends. I thank God with each prayer for bringing you into our lives."

Julie hugged her then whispered, "I'm still scared."

"I know, *liebling*. Pray for God to remind you that He's always with you."

"With Daddy, too?"

Philip swallowed hard as tears glistened in his eyes.

"Of course." Aveline's voice remained calm, but Lucas could see how her hands shook. Had something happened while they were moving the barn? "We're all *kinder* of our Father God. It is through Him that we learn His lessons so we can try to live the life He wants for us. I know this may be difficult to understand."

Julie looked down at the stuffed goat she held. "No, it's not. It's simple. Believe in God and trust His love."

Hugging the girl, Aveline stood and threaded her way among the crowd of young seamstresses. She stepped off the porch. She held Lucas's eyes for a second before heading toward the chicken coop at the side of the yard.

Though she said nothing, Lucas murmured, "We should go with her, Philip."

The other man argued, "I should stay—"

"Julie's fine with the other kids. Aveline wants to tell us something she doesn't want your daughter to hear."

Philip took one lingering look at his daughter, then nodded. As they crossed the yard, his assistant came to join them. Neal started to talk about the moving process, but halted when his boss shot him a quelling glare. However, Philip didn't ask Neal to leave. It was a sign, Lucas decided, that Philip trusted his assistant.

As soon as they reached where Aveline stood on the far side of the coop, out of earshot of the others, she said, "Julie insists someone was watching us while the move was going on."

"There were a bunch of *Englischers* stopping to watch," Lucas said.

She shook her head. "I mentioned that, but she told me to look at the trees where the creek runs by Annalise's farm."

"Did you see someone?" Lucas asked.

"I think so." She drawled the words as if unsure of them. "I didn't see anyone move, but Julie insisted the person had binoculars because she saw sunlight glinting off the lenses."

Neal gasped. "Binoculars?"

Philip waved him to silence. "Is she sure of what she saw?"

"*She* is sure."

"You're not?"

Wrapping her arms around herself, she said, "I wish I could be. She's always honest with us. Why would she lie about something like that?"

Lucas needed to be forthright. "She's scared. Maybe fear fired her imagination."

"I believe her, Lucas."

Philip's face grew pale under his tan. "I don't like this. You've been great, but I can't take the chance that something else will happen. Last time you saved her. I can't count on that a second time."

"The man who took her is in jail," Aveline said.

"We know he doesn't have the brains to come up with scheme on his own. Someone hired him." He snorted his derision. "Someone too cheap to find a henchman with the smarts to follow orders."

Without another word, Philip strode away. He stopped to collect a protesting Julie from the porch and led her away. A low buzz of questions erupted as soon as they disappeared past the house.

"He's overwrought," Neal said, staring after his boss. "I've never seen him so paranoid. He needs to snap out of it."

"Why?" Aveline demanded. "His daughter *was* abducted."

He scowled at her. "At least he has his daughter. My ex-wife refuses to let me see my kids." Reaiming his frown in Lucas's direction, he hurried to catch up with his boss.

Aveline clasped her hands in front of her. "Dear Lord, bring Neal and Philip healing. Take their anger and fill their hearts with hope."

"Amen," said Lucas.

"Do you think Philip will let Julie return?"

He had to be honest, though he knew the words would be as painful for her to hear as for him to say. "I don't know."

Chapter Thirteen

Lucas wiped his forehead with a blue bandana as he stood between the ruddy rows of potatoes. If the cloth left streaks of dirt among the sweat, he didn't care. It was as hot as a blacksmith's forge out in the fields, but his latest check had confirmed what he'd expected. The potatoes were ready.

He took another swipe at his nape. He wouldn't have been surprised if he could have fried an egg on top of his straw hat. What would the weather be like tomorrow? He scanned the western sky, but no hint of clouds broke the unblemished blue. No rain meant the heat wouldn't diminish. On the other hand, rain would make the harvest difficult. The harvester wouldn't work well in the mud. They'd discovered that last year when trying, after a downpour, to continue working.

Tomorrow, if it didn't rain, the earth would be

dry and crumbling when they tore the hills open and extracted the potatoes. He and Mark planned to begin in the smaller two fields that edged the creek dividing his farm from Mark's.

Heading toward his barns, Lucas winced as he moved his shoulders. Mark had been complaining earlier about his own abused muscles in the wake of carrying the woodworking shop onto Juan's farm. Yesterday, Lucas had been fine. In fact, he'd been so proud of that. Today, he wanted to get some liniment and bathe in it.

"That's what *hochmut* gets you," he said with a chuckle. "With pride comes pain."

His laugh disappeared as he came around the barn and saw a lone form by the goat pen. What was Julie doing there alone? Had she come to the farm on her own? He'd been certain Philip would refuse to let his daughter leave their house. Had she been driven in one of her *daed*'s cars? It was too far for the girl to walk on her own. He shuddered at the thought of how vulnerable she would have been crossing the Island on little-traveled roads.

"Hi, Lucas!" Julie called with a wave as he approached.

He started to return her greeting, then froze when he saw a motion in the deepest shadows beneath the maple tree at the edge of the lawn.

Aveline appeared, and he tamped down his anxiety before it became full-blown panic.

"You're right in time to celebrate with me," Lucas said as his and Aveline's paths converged beside Julie who was feeding the goats what looked like grapes.

"Celebrate what?" asked the enthusiastic *kind* before popping a couple of the green grapes into her mouth.

"The potato harvest can begin. We'll get started tomorrow."

"That's great news, Lucas," Aveline said as she handed Julie more grapes. "Make sure you don't give the goats anything but the fruit. They could choke on the stems."

"I know." Julie rolled her eyes as she laughed.

Lucas was astonished when Aveline took his arm and pulled him away from the *kind*. The firm hold of her fingers sent sweet pleasure flowing through him, but he ignored it as she said, "We need to talk. Alone."

Going with her to sit on the porch where they could keep an eye on Julie and not be heard, he said, "I didn't think she'd be back."

"I didn't either. I was shocked when Juan stopped by with her this morning and asked me to watch her. He's got an appointment with a *doktor* in Charlottetown, and he didn't want to leave her with just *Grossmammi* Fern to watch over her. *Mamm* wasn't happy about me agreeing to have Julie at our house, so I brought her over here."

He silenced his annoyance with Chalonna and her single-minded determination to let nobody get in the way of her plans.

"Did she tell Juan why she's come back?" he asked.

"Julie told me her *daed* was tired of her complaining about being stuck in their house. When she said she wanted to see her friends, he relented."

"I don't understand."

"He wants Julie to be happy, and it hurts him to make her sad."

"But he fears for her safety."

She shrugged. "She was taken from near their house, not from around here. Remember?"

"I hadn't thought of that. Though she was found on this side of the Island, there never has been any solid evidence she's being stalked over here."

"Exactly."

When Julie shouted she needed more grapes, Lucas went with Aveline to the pen. Aveline drew some more grapes from under her apron and handed the girl a bunch. The goats pressed against the fence to get their share.

"You're going to spoil them with this attention," he said in a mock scold. "What are they going to do when you go to school?"

Julie let out an ear-shattering wail. The grapes fell into the pen while she ran into the house and slammed the door.

"What did I say?" he asked as he snatched up the grapes before the goats got them.

Aveline sighed. "She told me her *daed* has arranged for her to go a private girls' boarding school in Toronto. That's why he went there last week before the barn was moved."

"He wants to send her so far from home?" He pulled the fruit off the stems and tossed the green balls into the pen to the goats.

"He's going to be spending a lot of time there, and he believes he'll see her more often that way. Also, he's leery of having her going to and from school here. Julie doesn't see it that way. She's made friends, and she doesn't want to leave. I know how she feels."

"You do?" he asked, surprised because Aveline so seldom spoke about her life before she came to the Island.

She rested her arms on top of the fence. "I had to leave so many people behind in Ontario."

"Family?"

"*Ja.*"

"Friends?"

"Of course."

"Someone who was more than a friend?"

She tilted her chin as she gave him a look from the corner of her eye. He didn't need to ask her what it meant. Her expression suggested he'd lost any sense he'd ever had to ask such a question.

Her voice became emotionless. "I left everyone behind, Lucas. Not like you. You brought members of your family with you. That must have been a relief. To know you didn't have to start from square one with building your community."

"I thought it would, but I've questioned my decision to ask them to join me. My cousins and my brother have gone through a lot to make their homes on the Island."

"I know, but Mark's barn has been rebuilt and is strong enough to stand up to any blizzard. Your brother has regained almost all his vision. Mattie and Daisy have made the farm shop into a success. Your farm is doing well." She stared at the fields. "You've got family here. We've only got us."

"Your family will be expanding with your brothers' marriages."

"It's not the same."

"Do you want to return to Ontario?"

She looked startled at what he'd considered an obvious question. For a long moment, she didn't answer him. The silence wore on and on until he wished he'd never asked the question, but how was he to know that such a commonplace query would make her mute?

It should have been as easy to answer the question as it had the others. There had been days when Aveline had ached to return to Ontario. Now she too often felt like the Confederation Bridge, spanning the distance between Prince Edward Island and the mainland. She could have answered Lucas's question by telling him about Merle. She could have, but what would she have said? It wasn't as if Merle had hinted about getting married. In fact, he'd been dismissive of friends who were thinking about it.

"Fools!" Merle had laughed while driving her home after a fudge-making frolic. "Why tie yourself down when you can have fun?"

"Maybe they've had enough fun." Her reply had been silly. She'd known that at the time but had been startled by his vehemence. She'd blurted out the first thing that had come to mind.

"Enough for a lifetime?"

"You don't think people have fun after they're married?" She hadn't been able to see his face. He could have turned on a lantern inside the buggy, but he never did. She hadn't figured out why, and he hadn't explained.

"I don't think most people do. They get bogged down in families and work."

"Families can be fun."

"Is yours?"

She hadn't answered. There wasn't any reason to because he'd known how strained everything was at home. At the time, she hadn't understood why her parents were on tenterhooks, but found out a month later when *Daed* had announced they were moving to Prince Edward Island the following week. She'd barely found time to tell Merle about the plans *Mamm* and *Daed* had made before their household was packed and a passenger van arrived to take them east. Merle had only wished her well.

Instead of answering Lucas's question, she said, "You've been kind to Julie."

"It's easy to do because she's a nice girl." He pushed away from the fence. Frustration burned in his eyes but he didn't pursue the question she'd ignored as he walked toward the house. "Sometimes it's easy to forget there are nice people in the world."

Her eyes widened in astonishment. "You usually aren't cynical, Lucas."

"I didn't ever used to be cynical at all."

"What happened?"

"Robin Boshart." He stopped in the middle of his yard, fingering the grape stems.

"Who's that?"

"Before I arrived on the Island, if someone had asked me such a question, I would have hemmed and hawed on an answer."

Common sense warned her not to probe but she asked, "Why?"

"Because I wouldn't have been able to decide whether to list Robin's *wunderbaar* qualities or to start with the one thing that hadn't been *wunderbaar*."

"What was that?" When she saw his shoulders stiffen, she said, "You don't have to tell me."

He looked at her as if for the first time. His eyes swept across her face before meeting her own. Her skin tingled as if he'd run his fingers along her cheek and her lips parted though no sound emerged.

"What wasn't *wunderbaar* was how she dumped me. She dumped me because I wasn't any fun to be around."

"You? Not fun? Everyone always laughs with you."

"She thought I was a stick in the mud."

"She said that? That's cruel."

"But honest."

"No, not honest. Cruel. You aren't a stick in the mud. You're kind and thoughtful." Sudden understanding burst through her. "Is *she* the reason

why you've been flirting with every woman?"
Every woman but me.

"I thought if I could prove I was fun—"

"Prove to whom? A woman who pushed you aside and is almost two thousand kilometers away? How does that make any sense?"

"It doesn't, but it was the only solution I had." He tossed the grape stems onto the porch before jamming his hands into his pockets. "If I changed myself, I wouldn't ever have to be told I was as much fun as a lump on a log. So I threw myself into being the new version of myself."

"Which worked. Everyone likes you."

"But I don't like myself. I spent a lot of years being the other version of myself, and I miss the original Lucas."

"You don't have to stay the new Lucas."

"I don't think I can." He put his hand on her arm and drew her a half step closer. "It's becoming too much effort to be everyone's buddy and try to make everybody laugh."

"Then why do it?"

"Aren't we what others expect us to be?"

She shook her head. "I don't think that's how God intends us to spend our lives. The only expectations we should meet are His." Catching his gaze, she almost bit back her next words when she saw the grief in his eyes. "What expectations do you think God has for you, Lucas?"

He didn't answer, and she wondered if he intended to ignore her question as she had his.

Knowing she was treading on unstable ground if she pushed him about his past without revealing hers, she said, "I can't deride you for being foolish when I've been the same."

"About what?"

"Listening to my *mamm*." She bent to retie her left sneaker. Not that it had needed to be done, but it was an excuse not to look at him and having him discover she was still avoiding his other question. "I've let my *mamm* convince me I'm nothing if I'm alone. That I'm less than half of a whole. No wonder she believes I'm a useless, ungrateful daughter."

"You've honored your parents by being a devoted and hardworking daughter. You love them, and they know it."

"Not every day." She couldn't hide her wry grin as the conversation turned away from Merle. "There have been days when I'm sure they've questioned how such a stubborn daughter has any love or respect for them."

"You're exaggerating."

"Maybe. A little bit."

"A little exaggeration is *gut* if it helps you heal."

"Do you think it would work for Julie and Philip?"

"I don't know what we could exaggerate to ease their grief and fear."

"Let's think about it." She smiled. "Philip said we're a *gut* team. We are, ain't so?"

"We are." He kissed her cheek, startling her. That amazement dissolved into a more potent emotion as he drew back, his gaze holding hers so she couldn't look away.

She didn't want to look away. She wanted to sink into the mysteries of his dark eyes, float there until each one opened itself to her, letting her come closer to the man he hid.

He slanted toward her until her smallest finger couldn't have fit between them. "Aveline..."

She waited for him to say something else, anything that would send his words across her lips in a heated caress. She murmured his name, but everything else vanished as his finger guided her chin to him.

His mouth on hers was gentle, urging her to share this pleasure with him. Everything she'd ever been told about a kiss, everything she'd ever read, paled in comparison to his mouth against hers. When her arm curved along his shoulders, he tugged her to him. His kiss deepened, thrilling her. She combed her fingers through the hair at his nape while he scattered kisses over her cheek and along her jaw. When he pressed his face to hers, his breath, uneven and warmer than the day's heat, swirled against her ear.

"Hey, Lucas!" came a shout.

Aveline jumped. Or had it been Lucas pulling back? It didn't matter. The wondrous moment was shattered.

"It's Mark," he said as if in apology.

"I know."

"I've got to go."

"I know."

"Aveline—"

Whatever he'd been going to say went unsaid because Mark called, waving his arms over his head, "Let's go. I want to check out the south field."

"I've got to get to work." Lucas didn't look at her, or so she assumed because she was keeping her eyes lowered, not wanting to see his expression. She didn't want to know the truth. Was he upset because it hadn't been the woman named Robin in his arms? Or was he bothered that it had been Aveline?

"I know," she whispered. "You've got a lot of harvesting ahead of you and, who knows? It could rain tomorrow."

She hated babbling about inconsequential matters, but to speak of what was in her heart was impossible. He hurried to meet his cousin. The two vanished from sight, but she remained where she was until sometime later—she had no idea how long—Julie reappeared from the house, her cheeks covered with the remnants of her tears.

It took every bit of Aveline's will not to let her own fall.

Chapter Fourteen

Aveline steered the buggy onto the road leading away from Montague. Bagel's clip-clops and the sound of the steel wheels on the asphalt were the only sounds. Beside her, Julie was curled into a ball of despair. Aveline's plan to take the *kind* to Montague to enjoy a cool drink on such a hot day had been a disaster from the beginning.

The harbor had been dull in the dim light sifting through clouds and humidity. Julie hadn't showed any interest in it. Aveline had thought the girl would like seeing the water that bisected Montague. The harbor by the bridge was wide enough for a boat to moor on either side, leaving space down the middle for another to pass. Beyond the marina, the water narrowed into a creek. On one side, the ground sloped along Rue Main. The other was filled with a collection of sculptures and unique art. A building covered with painted quilt squares was set next to shops selling books and T-shirts and *kaffi* to tourists.

Julie hadn't said a word while Aveline tried to keep a conversation going with her friend Valetta, whom they'd chanced to meet there. Valetta had been eager to talk about her upcoming wedding. It hadn't been only Julie's dreary feelings that had soured the conversation.

Aveline's own spirits had been bogged down. While Valetta spoke of her wedding to Wes, Aveline couldn't keep from thinking about Lucas. Had she made the biggest mistake of her life when she let Lucas kiss her?

"You're quiet today," Valetta had said as they'd crossed over the bridge to where Aveline had left her buggy. "Both of you."

Julie had burst into tears.

"Did I say something wrong?" Valetta had gasped.

Putting her arm around the girl's shoulders, Aveline had soothed Julie and Valetta. Julie had shot her a grateful look when Aveline didn't answer Valetta's question. Telling Valetta about how Julie was being sent to a boarding school far from the Island wasn't her story to share.

What a burden for a *kind* to bear! At some point, they had to let Evie and Daisy and the rest of Lucas's family know Julie wouldn't be visiting until Christmas. Hearing Philip mention she might be in Prince Edward Island over a fall break and seeing his bleak expression had warned Aveline it was unlikely the girl would return then.

The visit to the harbor hadn't done anything to lighten Julie's mood. Nor her own. She hadn't been surprised when Valetta had excused herself to finish her errands. As Julie hadn't showed any interest in a cold drink, though the air was heavy and the temperature rising, Aveline had decided it was time for them to leave as well.

As they drove along, passing fields where potatoes were being dug on both sides of the road, Aveline wondered how the harvest was going for Lucas. He wouldn't have a big potato digger like the *Englisch* used. Those ripped the potatoes out of their hills and dumped them into waiting trucks. Instead, his horse-drawn harvester with long, thin metal fingers opened the hills and freed the potatoes. His cousins would take turns with him driving the horses and picking up the potatoes by hand, then putting them in a wagon.

The smells of damp earth filled each breath because the thickening mist rising from the river held everything close to the ground. Fog was beginning to curl among the trees but the asphalt remained clear.

When the buggy turned onto the road leading past her family's farm, Aveline could take no more of Julie's painful silence. The way was empty ahead of them. A car rumbled behind them, but not close.

"Julie, would you like to try driving the buggy?" she asked.

"What's the point?" grumbled the girl. "There aren't any buggies in Toronto."

Praying Julie's heart could somehow be comforted, she said, "You're planning to come and visit us when you're on the Island, ain't so?"

"Can I?" She raised her head for the first time since they'd left Montague.

"Of course. You know we'd love to see you whenever you can join us."

"For work frolics?"

Aveline smiled. "There's always work that needs to be done."

"You won't let anyone move another building unless I'm here, will you?"

"If someone needs to move a building, I'll find out where and when and let your *daed* know."

"You promise?"

Nodding, Aveline wondered how many promises had been made and broken to the *kind*. "Ready to try the reins?"

"Yes!" Julie listened as Aveline showed her how to hold the reins, making sure they were secure so she wouldn't lose control if something spooked the horse. Not that Aveline needed to worry about that with Bagel. The horse was the calmest she'd ever driven. Left on his own, he could have found his way to his stall without any guidance.

"That's right," Aveline said as she let Julie hold the reins on her own. "Don't try to steer. Bagel knows these roads, and he's the best judge of where to go. Horses are smarter than many people give them credit for. He'll make sure we don't hit a pothole or something abandoned in the road."

"Look at me!" Julie wore a big grin. "I'm doing it!"

"*Ja*, you are." She heard a car approaching from beyond the corner ahead. The fog hid the edges of the road, but she knew there was a deep ditch on each side. "Draw Bagel a bit to the right so the car has room, but trust him to find the way."

Julie had barely enough time to do that before the car sped past them in the other lane. Its wheels slid over the center line as it rounded the corner.

"They're driving too fast. Fools!" Julie spat.

"It's better we pray they learn restraint so they don't hurt themselves or others." Despite her words, Aveline frowned as she looked over her shoulder at where the car had already disappeared into the thickening fog.

"Randall says the same thing." The girl chuckled. "Though he doesn't say it so nicely. You're a nice person, Aveline."

"I try to be."

"That's why Lucas likes you, you know. He likes you because you're nice."

Aveline knew she must have said something to Julie, because the girl continued guiding Bagel along the road, but Aveline couldn't remember the words as soon as she spoke them. Lucas wouldn't think she was so nice when he discovered she'd been false with him about whom she'd left behind in Ontario. He'd been honest with her about the woman who'd tossed him aside. Aveline had evaded his questions.

And he'd let her.

If she'd needed proof he wasn't the careless, carefree man who flirted with every woman he'd met, unmindful of the hurt he might leave behind...there it was. He'd opened himself by telling her the ugly truth. She hadn't been able to do the same, though her situation with Merle must have been different from Lucas's with Robin. Merle had been her friend. Nothing more. She had to admit that. Lucas hadn't hidden he'd had deep feelings for Robin, that he'd believed the breakup was his fault and he'd tried to change, but wasn't happy with the man he'd become. She'd wallowed in her disappointment, when, if she'd been honest, she knew there hadn't been any future for her and Merle. He'd become an excuse for her to avoid any relationships with men, to prefer being a victim when there hadn't been any crime.

She and Lucas had wasted their lives, trying to be what they thought they should be instead of embracing the life God had given them.

The next time she ran into Lucas—No! She was going to head to his house tonight after supper and tell him the truth. Though she had no idea what might happen, she knew it was the right thing to do. For herself, for him, for both of them.

"Aveline!" Julie's sharp cry sliced into Aveline's thoughts. "Aveline! Aveline!"

"*Was iss letz?*" she asked, then repeated in English, "What's wrong?"

"That car! Why is it slowing down? Isn't it the same one that passed us going so fast?"

Aveline gasped when she realized a car was keeping pace with the buggy, driving the wrong way. Julie was right. It was the same car.

Taking the reins, Aveline gave them a quick slap. The horse picked up his pace, but the vehicle could match their speed, no matter what it was. A single horse-powered buggy couldn't outrun a car.

Suddenly the car sped forward. Aveline started

to release her breath, glad it was going to pass them. That breath exploded out in a cry when the car skidded around in front of them. It was in their lane, cutting off Bagel. The horse whinnied in fear. He tried to rise on his hind legs, but the harness prevented that. Instead, he began backing away. Their rear wheel struck the edge of the road, and the buggy teetered. Julie cried out in horror.

Aveline tightened her hold on the reins until the leather cut into her palms. She jammed her foot on the buggy's brake, hoping to keep them from tipping over and falling into the roadside ditch. That could leave her and Julie injured, but it might leave Bagel with a broken leg. A death sentence for a buggy horse.

Then the buggy stopped. It remained upright.

"*Danki*, God," Aveline whispered as she gathered the trembling girl in her arms. Her heart pounded in her ears. "*Danki* for keeping us safe."

Julie cried out in the moment before the girl was jerked away from Aveline. Looking past the *kind*, Aveline gasped.

Two men wearing ski masks stood on the road. One held Julie, who was struggling to get away. He raised his hand to strike her, but Aveline slid out and grasped his arm.

Her own arm was seized, then twisted behind her until she moaned with pain. She planted her feet in time to keep from being shoved into the side of the car.

A third man jumped out and opened the back door on the driver's side. Like the others, he wore a mask to conceal his face. He motioned for Aveline to get into the car.

"No," she said with the tattered rags of her courage. If she got in the car, she wasn't sure she'd get out alive.

Julie's captor pushed her forward, and Julie flung her arms around Aveline. The *kind*'s frantic motion shoved her away from her own captor. "Do what he says," the *kind* whispered. "He's got a gun."

Aveline caught the glint in one of the men's hands and nodded. She put her arm around Julie, maneuvering herself between the girl and the gun.

"C'mon, lady. Get in the car. Don't make us shoot you and the kid." A man grabbed Julie's arm and tried to pull her away from Aveline. The girl let out a screech, and the man froze for a moment.

It was all the time Aveline had. And, she prayed, all she needed.

Jumping backward, she stuck her arm between Julie and the man. She must have startled him because he recoiled. As she'd hoped he would.

Yanking Julie away, she shoved the girl toward the buggy. "Go!"

Julie cried, "Come with me, Aveline! C'mon!"

"I'm coming!"

Trying to disentangle her arm from the man's, she pushed against his chest. He tottered backward. Mud splashed out of the ditch as he toppled in.

Hands stretched for her. She ran along the shoulder, avoiding them. She reached the buggy as Julie was climbing in and grasping for the reins. It began to move as Julie shouted to her to get in.

The men tried to get between her and the buggy. Julie was trying to drive it past the car.

"No!" Aveline shrieked and ran faster, though she hadn't known she could.

A man blocked her way. He snarled a curse. A motion from the corner of her eye was her only warning before his fist struck the side of her head. She hadn't guessed people really saw stars, but sparkles danced in front of her eyes. Then they vanished…along with everything else in the world, leaving her with her prayer that Julie had escaped.

Clouds hung close to the ground. Fog had swirled in off the river, and Lucas felt rain spit in his face. The pleasant sunny days of summer would soon be replaced by the stormy days of fall. In quick order, snow would arrive to slow the pace of life on the Island.

Though it wasn't chilly, he shivered with the damp. He prayed the cold would stay away until he got his potatoes out of the fields. Mark had already negotiated the sale of most of their crop to the processor that bought a large portion of the Island's potatoes. They would be peeled, cut, and made into French fries and other convenience foods before being frozen and shipped throughout Canada and the United States. A much smaller portion of the potatoes had been set aside to sell at the family's farm shop, and less would remain in the darkest, coolest part of the potato storage barn for Mark's and his own use through the winter.

First they needed to get all the potatoes out of their hills. The work had been going well until one of the metal strips on the harvester had broken into three pieces. After a quick drive into Shushan, he had a handful of replacements in his buggy. He'd bought the harvester used, a barn find left in a dusty corner when the farmer had moved on to using a tractor-pulled harvester. It'd been a bargain, but he'd known the upkeep would be ongoing.

He heard a plane overhead and twisted to look up. Maybe that was Philip returning from his latest business trip. His daughter would be thrilled to see her *daed*. Lucas couldn't figure out how a man who worried so much about his daughter's safety could fly hundreds of kilometers away at the drop of a hat.

If not for Aveline's attentions to Julie this past week, the girl would be stuck in that huge house, afraid and alone.

Aveline... Her name brought the image of her face so close to his in the second before he'd kissed her. He'd never imagined a freckled face and bright red hair would become integral parts of his dreams.

Had he been wrong to kiss her when she'd made it clear marriage wasn't in her plans?

The question had lingered since that marvelous moment when he'd held her close. The anguish of being dumped by Robin had vanished as if it'd never existed. Everything he'd suffered had been a waste of time. Instead of reminding himself everyone had a right to their opinion— no matter how mistaken—he'd accepted Robin's words as the truth.

"No," he said aloud, "I wasn't wrong to kiss Aveline when I had the chance. My mistake was not doing it sooner. Or again instead of being so spooked by Mark's arrival." He hadn't wanted Aveline put in an embarrassing spot of being discovered in his arms, but how tough it'd been to let her go. "Okay, I messed up."

The horse's ears twitched. In reaction to his voice or to something else?

He had to laugh at his own discombobulation. How ironic that he had a reputation for ricocheting from one woman to another without a care in the world! The reality was he couldn't get his feet under him and deal with a single one. If—

Rebel's abrupt neigh broke into Lucas's thoughts. His horse pulled toward the right shoulder. What was going on? The horse was upset. But by what?

Lucas squinted through the wisps of fog flowing along the road like phantom rabbits. A shape, dark and boxy, began to emerge through the mist.

A buggy!

He strained his eyes, but couldn't see anyone near it. Who'd left a buggy by the side of the road? Was it broken down?

As Lucas drove closer, he didn't see any damage to the vehicle. He started to call out, but refrained when the buggy rolled forward a few feet. Then he realized it was starting and stopping as if the horse wasn't sure what to do. Jumping out, he raced toward the other horse. It shied and stamped its forefoot. That was, Lucas knew, a signal the horse wanted to leave.

"It's going to be okay," Lucas crooned as he

stroked the anxious animal. Running his hand forward along the horse's shoulders, he kept talking in a low, quiet voice. Then he recognized the animal. "Bagel?"

The horse's ears flicked at its name.

"What are you doing here on your own?" he asked before peering into the buggy. It was empty except for a black purse on the seat.

What was going on? Aveline wouldn't abandon her horse by the side of the road. If she'd gotten out, wouldn't he have seen her when he passed? Why would she leave her purse in plain sight on the seat? She wasn't careless like that.

He frowned. Wasn't she supposed to be spending the afternoon with Julie?

"Aveline?" he shouted. "Julie?"

His voice was swallowed by the fog. Straining his ears, he heard nothing but the two horses and his own unsteady breathing. Again, he called their names.

Again, he heard nothing.

Stepping away from Bagel, he edged to the side of the road. He halted when one of his feet slid down a slope. The ditch was filled with water. He stopped, cupped his mouth and bellowed Aveline's and Julie's names as loud as he could. He waited for a response, listening to his heartbeat hammer.

Nothing.

Then he saw two black lines left by tires on the road behind the buggy. The car that had made them must have been in a hurry. A big hurry. He ran over to where the tire marks burst out from the side of the road.

Footprints were visible by the side of the road. Sickness clamped on to him when he saw smaller footprints among the big ones. Small enough for Aveline's feet and for Julie's.

A car had zipped past the buggy and turned at a high speed. Why?

The answer was horrifying. They'd feared Trace hadn't been alone in his plan to abduct Julie. What would his confederates have dared to make sure their kidnapping was successful this time?

The thought jolted him into motion. Tying Bagel's lines to his buggy, he climbed in and gave Rebel the order to go. It wasn't far to the Lampels'. He hoped he could get there in time to get the help he needed.

A cramp in his gut told him he had to hurry. Time might be running out fast for Aveline and Julie.

Chapter Fifteen

Lucas stopped both buggies in the Lampels' farm lane. He wasn't out of his before Aveline's brothers rushed through the drizzle. Wes ran to him while Dwayne paused, staring at the linked buggies.

"Did you see them?" Dwayne shouted. "Do you know where they went?"

"I don't know," he said, astonished word of Aveline and Julie's disappearance had reached the Lampels' farm before him. "I found her buggy empty on the highway. Has anyone contacted Philip DeSare?"

Wes scowled as he neared. "Philip? What are you talking about? Why would we contact an *Englischer* about our missing water buffalo? Did you see them out on the road? If…" He squinted through the fog. "Hey, that's Aveline's buggy. Why do you have it hooked to yours?"

Questions about the missing water buffalo teased him, but Lucas paid them no attention. He told Aveline's brothers what he'd discovered out on the main road. They peered into the buggy, hoping they'd see something he'd missed. He reached into his buggy and drew out her purse.

"This was the only thing in it," he said.

Before either man could answer, the sound of an auto engine rumbled in the distance, coming closer. Misty headlights emerged, followed by Philip's sleek black car. As Philip stepped out, Aveline's *daed* burst from the fog in the opposite direction.

"Why are you boys standing around when the herd is out there somewhere?" Elam asked as his wife moved beside him.

Lucas said nothing while he handed Aveline's purse to Chalonna. She looked past him toward the interconnected buggies, then at Philip's car.

"Where's my daughter?" she demanded.

"I don't know," Lucas said.

Chalonna pointed her finger at Philip as he stepped out of his car. "I knew it was a mistake to let you into our house the first day you came here. I tried to talk sense to Aveline, but she couldn't see how having *Englischers* in our lives was sure to cause trouble." She whirled on Lucas. "You're around her too much. How—"

Elam silenced her with a sharp, "Enough,

Chalonna. This isn't the time or the place." When she gawped at him in disbelief, he said in a gentler voice, "Take Aveline's purse inside, so it doesn't get lost. We're going to need a lot of food and drink before this is over. Will you prepare it for us?"

"Before what is over?" she asked, fear growing in her eyes.

"I don't know," Lucas repeated.

She stared at him for a long minute before, clutching the purse to her chest, she walked into the house. No one spoke until they heard the door close behind her.

"Dwayne, go and help your *mamm*," Elam ordered, his gaze riveted on Lucas.

"*Daed—*"

"She needs your help."

Aveline's brother nodded and followed his *mamm* inside.

"What's happened?" Elam asked.

Lucas started to share the few facts he had. He halted and turned to Philip. "You know more, ain't so?"

"I know Aveline and Julie are in danger," the *Englischer* said. "Because of this." He drew a piece of paper out from under his suit coat and thrust it into Lucas's hand.

Opening it, he almost recoiled as he saw the letters cut from magazines and newspapers. Each word, except Julie's name, was made of individually pasted letters. His stomach twisted tighter when he realized whoever had created the note must have pulled her name from periodicals reporting how she'd gone missing the first time.

The message was terse and right to the point. If the police were contacted, the *kind* would be killed. There was no mention of Aveline, which he should have expected. The kidnappers, because it must have been more than one to snatch both Aveline and Julie, couldn't have known they'd be abducting two people when they'd put the note together.

He passed it to Elam, who read it along with his son. They became ashen as Aveline's *daed* handed the page to Philip, who folded it and returned it to his pocket.

"So where are they?" Wes asked, looking from one man to the next.

Lucas said, "The fishing hut!"

"What?" Philip clenched his hands at his sides. "What fishing hut?"

"Julie mentioned when she was kidnapped the f-f-first t-t-time," he said, unable to stop his voice from shaking. He took a steadying breath. "When Julie was taken the first time, the guy tried to get her to go with him to a fishing hut. It might have been a rendezvous point for the kidnappers."

"A hut?" Elam shook his head. "There must be hundreds along the Island's shores."

"It has to be close by. Whoever gave Trace his orders had to have recognized the man couldn't deal with anything complicated. The hut can't be far from where we found Julie."

"There's that old hut on the far side of the cove. Across from the holiday cottages," Wes said.

"Upriver or down?" Lucas asked.

"Downriver. It's between the marsh and the river. I remember seeing it once when Dwayne and I were kayaking. I assume it's still there."

Philip groaned. "Between the marsh and the river? We can't get there without making a lot of noise. If they hear us coming, they could turn on their captives."

Lucas put his hand on Philip's quivering shoulder. "Then we have to mask our approach."

"How? As foggy as it is out there, we'll be bumbling about trying not to run into trees or fall into the swamp."

Before he could answer, the clatter of hooves on the road flowed out of the fog. The herd of water buffalo strolled into sight as if they went for a walk beyond their field every day.

Elam and his son took a single step toward them, and the herd backed away, breaking apart. The men paused, and the water buffalo bunched.

Elam took a single step, and they turned, ready to run.

"Aveline calls them to her by saying 'treat-treat-treat,'" Lucas said. "They rush right over to her to get an alfalfa cube."

Sending Wes to get some cubes from the barn, Elam didn't move until his son returned. They coaxed the water buffalo toward the field.

"Wait a minute!" Turning to Elam, Lucas said, "I've got an idea. You may not like it, but it's an idea."

"Tell us!" urged Philip.

"Moobeam."

"What?" asked everyone but Elam at the same time.

Aveline's *daed* stared at Lucas. Did Elam think he'd lost his mind or was so desperate he'd grasp at any solution, no matter how ridiculous?

"What's a Moobeam?" asked Philip.

"One of Aveline's water buffalo calves."

It was Philip's turn to glare at him. "This is absurd, Lucas. I've heard all I care to hear. I'm going to—"

"You should listen to Lucas," Elam said with quiet dignity before Lucas could speak. "He's got a *gut* head on his shoulders, so he must have a *gut* reason for such a suggestion."

Lucas hid his shock at Elam's words. Later, once Aveline and Julie were safe, he'd let himself be astonished. "It's simple." Then he explained his idea.

The skepticism on the other faces became hope as one, then another, then all nodded. He prayed their faith in him wouldn't be betrayed. He tried not to think of how a single miscalculation in the toughest decision he'd ever had to make would mean Aveline and Julie paying the price for him being wrong.

A headache threatened to blind Aveline, but she ignored it. She sat on the filthy floor of a tiny hut that reeked of water and mildew and sweat. Water sloshed under the uneven wooden floors, so she guessed they were perched over the river. Or was it the ocean? She couldn't be sure.

Julie leaned against her, sobbing, but Aveline couldn't put her arms around the *kind*. Her wrists were lashed together behind her. Feeling had vanished from her fingers.

She watched the three men guarding them. In her mind, one was "Deer-Guy" because of the red deer on his mask, and the other was "Snowflake," for the same reason. The third mask didn't have any distinctive marks except a small rectangle that she guessed was a designer's label, so she called the man "Blue" to match the color of the mask.

The three men were arguing as they had been

for the last half hour. Not that she could discern their words because they had their backs to her and the *kind*, but their postures were aggressive and angry. She prayed their fury wouldn't be unleashed in her and Julie's direction.

Was one of them the mastermind behind both kidnappings? He must be. Wouldn't he have learned his lesson with leaving someone else guarding his captives? Trace had failed the first time. Maybe these men weren't so witless.

She shuddered, knowing smart criminals wouldn't be *gut* for her and Julie.

"Aveline?" murmured Julie, raising her head.

"It's going to be all right," she whispered.

"Is it?"

"God is here with us. Don't forget that."

There was a pause before Julie said, "I'll try not to, but it's hard."

"I know. Faith is hard. If—"

The men whirled as something jolted the hut. Snowflake rushed to the sole window.

"There are buffalo out there!" he shouted.

"Buffalo?" sneered Blue, and she felt Julie stiffen against her. Did she recognize the man's voice? It seemed familiar, but Aveline couldn't place it, not even when he said, "You're seeing things."

The hut shook and dust fell from the rafters onto Aveline's *kapp*.

"Look for yourself!" Snowflake motioned to the window. As the hut was struck a third time, his face went as white as the yarn in his ski mask. "They're going to stampede right through here and kill us!"

Aveline started to stand to peer out the window. Had the water buffalo escaped? Were they outside the hut?

Julie jumped to her feet and shrieked, "Treat-treat-treat, Moobeam! Treat-treat-treat!"

Wood cried out as it cracked near the window. The men scrambled out of the way, tripping over their feet and each other.

"Treat-treat-treat, Moobeam!" Aveline shouted, with Julie echoing her.

A rafter came loose and swung down, just missing them. The men screamed in terror, but Aveline and Julie kept calling to the water buffalo calf.

When hands grabbed her, Aveline struggled to escape. It was impossible with her bound hands, but she kept trying until a familiar voice—a dear and familiar voice—said, "It's Lucas. We're here to get you two out."

She nodded, not bothering to ask who "we" was. Another dust cloud filled the hut, and she heard Moobeam's frustrated bawl. Moments later, she was out of the hut that was collaps-

ing behind her. Where was Julie? Was Moobeam
okay? Where were the kidnappers?

It took an hour for Aveline to learn the answers
to those questions. She sat on a folding chair
someone had found beneath the debris of the col-
lapsed hut that had partially sunk into the river.
With the ropes gone from her wrists, she winced
each time she moved her fingers. She held Julie
on her lap. The girl's feet brushed the ground, but
she nestled against Aveline like a *boppli*. Lucas
stood on one side of them, and Philip paced on
the other side. Wes had herded the water buffalo back to the farm, giving them treats as they
went. *Daed* had reassured her Moobeam hadn't
suffered any cuts from her eager entrance into
the fishing hut, but Aveline hadn't been satisfied
until she'd checked the calf herself.

At the edge of the cove where the hut sat along
the Brudenell River, their abductors were hand-
cuffed and in the backs of a trio of police cars.
Mamm hadn't listened. As soon as Lucas, *Daed*
and Wes had left with Philip and the herd, she'd
insisted Randall use his phone to call the RCMP,
outlining where her husband was leading the others and why. The police had arrived in time to
see everyone fleeing the hut.

"I can't believe it," Philip said for what must
have been the tenth time. "I trusted him. I tried
to help him. I was ready to promote him, and

he abducted my daughter." His voice hardened. "Twice!"

Aveline couldn't believe it, either, but when the police had yanked off the men's ski masks, she'd understood why Blue's voice had sounded familiar. Beneath the bright blue mask had been Neal Mathers's familiar features. She struggled to connect the quiet man, who'd seemed to care so much about his boss, with a kidnapper.

"What are the Mounties saying?" Julie whispered, drawing her attention to the *kind*.

"They're explaining to Neal and the others why they're being arrested."

"Don't they know?"

In spite of her exhaustion and headache, Aveline smiled. "You'd think so, but police officers must be exact. In case Neal and the others try to pull some prank in court."

"Will we have to go to court?"

"Let's wait and see." She didn't want the girl worrying.

Neal snarled an insult in their direction, and Philip exploded toward him. Lucas gave chase, halting Philip as he started to swing his fist at his former assistant. Aveline ran forward with Julie on her heels. The police stepped between them and the car, but were silent. She realized with astonishment they were waiting for Lucas to defuse the situation.

Philip's face looked as threatening as a thunderstorm. No signs of the debonair millionaire were visible. Only a furious *daed* who had meant it when he'd said he'd do anything to protect his daughter.

"He's not worth it," Lucas murmured as he drew Philip's hand down.

Philip cursed under his breath, then asked, "How can you say that? He and his henchmen terrorized Julie and Aveline." His hands curled into fists. "Beating him to a pulp is what he deserves."

"What he deserves is something a jury will determine," Aveline said. "Let God be his judge. God already knows what should become of him and the others."

"Listen to them, Mr. DeSare," said Constable Boulanger in a calming voice. "Don't let him provoke you into doing something that will get *you* in trouble. Can't you see that's what he wants?"

Spitting on the ground, Philip turned and walked away. He took his daughter's hand and kept walking.

The RCMP officer sighed before saying, "Thank you for waiting. You can go. We've got your initial statements. If it's okay with you, we'll visit your homes tomorrow and get an in-depth account from each of you."

Aveline nodded and turned to Lucas. Before

he could say a word, *Daed* put his arm around her as if she were no older than Julie.

"*Danki* for your help, Lucas. Her *mamm* and I won't ever forget it," *Daed* said before drawing her with him, away from the cars.

She waited for Lucas to say something but, for once, he was silent. What was wrong? Where was the glib Lucas Kuepfer who could talk to anyone about anything at any time?

That answer she didn't get and wondered if she ever would when he didn't follow as she and *Daed* headed away from the ruined hut.

As the three white vans with the DeSare company logo on the front doors were emptied, Lucas stepped forward to help his cousin Daisy out and into her wheelchair. He stopped, astonished, when he realized the third van was equipped with a lift that was lowering her chair to the driveway.

Daisy waved when her eyes were level with his. "Boppi Lynn says we need one of these for our buggy."

"We'd need a second buggy to carry around the battery to operate it." He laughed as she rolled onto the driveway and the lift began to go up. "It'd be so heavy, the front wheels would be high in the air. Imagine the poor horse that had to pull that."

Giggling, Daisy said, "Well, Boppi Lynn likes riding it anyhow."

"Tell her she has two more rides. One up here and another down when you get home."

"Yippee!" She pushed hard on her wheels and took off toward the house.

"She sounds ready to party," came a stern voice from behind him.

Lucas turned to see Aveline's *mamm* frowning at Daisy, who was already engaged in another conversation. This one with Randall, the man who'd been driving the accessible van. They were grinning.

That seemed to make Chalonna scowl more. He understood why when she grumbled, "I don't like our *kinder* being around everything these *Englischers* have. Mark my words. We'll have fewer baptisms if they're beguiled by these electronic gizmos."

"The *Englisch* world is always around us," he replied. Though he didn't want to argue with Chalonna, he couldn't stay silent. Maybe quarreling was a habit with him. He'd been debating with himself for the past week. To see Aveline and not speak of what filled his heart seemed almost as much of a torment as knowing she and Julie had been abducted. Knowing he should button his lip, he continued. "None of us grows up unaware of what's in the *Englisch* world."

"We don't push it upon our *kinder*."

He almost said that nobody was doing that and that Chalonna could have turned down Philip's invitation to a picnic at his house to celebrate his daughter's safe return. She wouldn't listen to a single word he said.

Lucas was glad he'd stayed silent when Aveline and her *daed* and brothers joined them. Then he wished he could find words. Ordinary words to greet them and not feel as if everything he said was wrong.

He needn't have worried. Wes and Dwayne chattered like a pair of squirrels as they gaped at Philip's grand house. They were in awe of the windows and the doors and the rooflines and its size. The fountain in front of the house had them getting down on their hands and knees to peer at the plumbing.

Though he considered staying with Aveline's brothers, he went to the front door with the rest of her family. Elam picked up the baskets his sons had been carrying and shoved them into Lucas's hands, motioning with his head for Lucas to follow Aveline. She hadn't looked at him since she'd stepped out of the van that had brought the Lampels to the estate. She remained silent, always keeping either her *mamm* or *daed* between them.

Lucas put the baskets on the kitchen island's

shining counter. Behind him, Chalonna breathed, "Oh, my!"

He waited for her to add something else, to point out what didn't meet her exacting standards. She didn't. Instead, she walked around the island, running her fingers along its top. When she got to the huge stove with its multitude of burners, she stared at it like a *kind* looking at a stack of candy bars.

"I've never seen you so impressed with anything, Chalonna." Elam chuckled. "Not even with one of us."

Aveline smiled. "As you've said many times, *Daed*, she's happiest when she's preparing food." She watched her *mamm* wander around the kitchen as if walking through a dream. "Wait until she sees the *kaffi* maker in the corner."

"She's going to want to try that out, especially if she can get a cappuccino. She loved the one she had in Montague."

"Did I hear someone mention a cappuccino?" asked Rodney as the bishop walked into the kitchen, bringing the faint scent of his blacksmith's forge with him. "I'm glad to see you looking so well." He gave them a wry grin. "I visited the jail yesterday with a local Methodist minister. We offered to speak to the men being held there. One agreed for us to pray with him. The one with a black eye. He said he got it from you, Aveline."

"He's right." A faint flush climbed her cheeks.

"You struck him?" her *daed* asked, dumb-founded.

"By accident. I didn't want him to put Julie in his car, so I tried to get between them. When he pushed me aside, I struggled to hold on to my balance. My arms flung out, and I must have struck him then." She lowered her eyes. "Oh, and I shoved one of them into a ditch. That wasn't an accident. He was trying to keep me from reaching the buggy."

"I should remind you," Rodney said as his lips twitched, "that violence isn't our way because it doesn't solve anything, but trying not to get knocked off your feet isn't violence. It's instinct. I'm sure God will forgive you for giving that man a bath."

"Something he probably needed," Lucas said.

For the first time that afternoon, Aveline met his gaze without looking away. He saw questions in her eyes, and he wanted to draw her aside and answer each one, no matter how difficult it would have been.

Instead, Julie and Philip entered the kitchen. He shook Lucas's hand so vigorously, Lucas feared his shoulder would break. The *Englischer* leaned forward and kissed Aveline's cheek.

"I'm not going to ask if it's okay for me to do that, bishop," Philip said with a broad smile in Rodney's direction. "My daughter was kidnapped. Twice. Aveline saved her. Twice. I think I'm owed at least this way to tell you thank you for all you've done for her." His voice broke as he added, "For both of us. I'll never be able to thank you enough." He hugged his daughter. "Neither of us will."

"No thanks are necessary," Lucas said. "We did what anyone else would have done."

"I know you believe that, but I can tell you that you're wrong." Anger slid across his face, then was gone.

Lucas knew what had happened would haunt Philip for the rest of his life. He prayed his *Englisch* friend would find a way to put it all behind him.

And that he could, too.

Aveline saw the pain in Philip's eyes and was glad when Julie insisted they come out onto the deck, which had a splendid view of the dunes. The change of scene might help the *Englischer* to put aside his pent-up fury long enough to enjoy the day. She wanted him to have happy memories instead of bad ones.

Philip hung back as her family and the bishop left to follow the girl. "Before you head outside," he said to her and Lucas, "I need to ask you something. I couldn't get this out earlier, so I'm going to try again." He cleared his throat. "As you know, we haven't resolved the issue with the reward I offered."

"Rodney told us that." Aveline glanced at Lucas. "He's kept us informed as much as he can."

"I'm sure he has." Philip nodded. "Rodney is a good man. I admire how much he cares for his community, doing all he can and expecting nothing in return."

"Other," Lucas replied, "than knowing God must be pleased he's doing a *gut* job."

Philip smiled. "You'd make a good bishop, Lucas. Have you thought about doing it?"

When Lucas looked abashed, Aveline said, "Philip, our next bishop will be chosen by lot from among our ordained men. Nobody would ever say they wanted the job. That would be a sure sign of *hochmut*. What you would call pride."

"I've got a lot to learn about you plain people." He rubbed his hands against his khaki trousers. "We've gotten off topic. I wanted to ask if you'd be willing to give the reward back to me." He forestalled their answers by adding, "Let me explain before you answer. Okay?"

Though Aveline wanted to express her gratitude Philip was willing to do as she hoped he would right from the beginning, she said, "Okay."

"Neal Mathers has been my friend for many

years. He was a good man, but changed when his wife filed for divorce. I'm not sure he was sorry to lose her. However, he was devastated to lose his children. It did something to his mind, and I think he focused his anger on me still having Julie." He shook his head as if he couldn't believe what he was saying. "I'd like to use the money I gave you to get him help. A psychiatrist who can guide him with talk therapy. It might be possible to get back the man he was."

"*Ja*," Lucas said.

"You're okay with returning the reward?"

"*Ja*," Aveline repeated, glancing at Lucas, whose gaze was affixed on Philip's face. An odd expression dimmed his eyes. She was curious why but didn't ask.

"Thank you!" Philip's smile returned. "I'm praying it'll make a difference in his life."

"We will be, too," she said.

Lucas nodded and headed for the door to the deck.

She hurried away in the opposite direction, not sure where she was going, but sure Lucas intended to shut her out of his life for a reason she couldn't guess.

Hours later, when the last of the food had been consumed and everyone was enjoying the pleasant afternoon warmth and talking about the harvest that was well underway, Aveline listened to Julie, Evie and Daisy talking and giggling together.

"What's so funny?" Aveline asked.

Julie pointed first to Mattie, then to each of the cousins as she said, "They were named for the old nursery rhyme."

"Which one?" Aveline asked, puzzled.

"The one that goes...

"Matthew, Mark, Luke and John,
Bless the bed that I lay on.
Four corners to my bed,
Four angels round me spread.
One at the head, one at the feet,
And two to guard me while I sleep."

She grinned. "Except you're Mattie, Mark, Lucas and Juan."

Aveline bit her lip to keep from laughing as the cousins looked at each other as if they'd never made the connection. She wondered how many times and in how many ways they'd heard something similar.

Lucas's voice held no hint of humor as he said, "Imagine that! I can't say I ever thought the four of us would be immortalized in a poem."

"It's not about you!" Julie jammed her hands onto her hips. "It's about the apostles. You just have the same names." She rolled her eyes. "Grown-ups! Sometimes you don't see what's right in front of you." Without a pause, she asked, "Did you hear? Daddy isn't making me go to boarding school. I'm going to go to school right here in Prince Edward Island where he says he can keep an eye on me. That's because he won't be traveling as much."

"That's *wunderbaar*, Julie." Aveline hugged the girl. "I'm happy for you and your *daed* and us because we'll get to see you often."

"Of course you will! Juan is going to teach me to play the harmonica, and Evie has promised to help me find a dog as nice as hers." She rattled off a long list of plans she had, some Aveline guessed Philip hadn't heard about yet.

Aveline let her laugh out when the girl ran off to play with Evie and Daisy, who wanted to visit Julie's room. When she heard giggles coming from the trio, her heart filled almost to bursting. Lucas and his family had opened their homes and their lives to Julie without question.

As they'd opened their homes and lives to her. Had they seen her loneliness?

But one of those doors remained closed.

Lucas's.

She didn't speak to anyone as she walked to the dunes and, after taking off her shoes and leaving them on a dune, out onto the beach where her shadow turned the red sand to a deeper shade.

The steady rhythm of the sea offered her a reminder of how God had created the world, having its beauty ready for moments when she needed comforting.

Another shadow moved toward hers, merging as Lucas came to stand beside her. He didn't say anything. Instead he reached out a single finger to slip it into her hand. When she didn't pull away, he wove his fingers through hers.

The silence between them was precious. Without words, they could linger in this time and place.

The dunes distorted the voices of the others by the house. As she walked with Lucas closer to the water, its soft motion on the sand concealed the rest of the noise from the house. They were left with the sounds of the sea and the calls of gulls who'd been drawn to the beach by aromas from the buffet.

"Julie is right," Lucas said as he faced her.

"About what?" She had to struggle to get out those two words as she fell into his dark brown eyes. She wasn't sure if she could escape. She wasn't sure she wanted to.

"That sometimes we overlook what's right in front of us." He curved his hand along her cheek. "For the past two years, I've been paying no attention to a sweet, *wunderbaar* woman who's been right in front of me."

"Don't," she said. "I'm not *wunderbaar*. I haven't been honest with you."

"About what?"

She took a deep breath and said, "There was a fellow I liked in Ontario. It broke my heart when I moved here and had to leave him behind. You asked me if there was someone there I missed, and I didn't answer you."

"Not answering is not the same as lying."

"I was afraid to tell you."

His brows lowered. "Afraid? Why?"

"Because I didn't want you to hear how foolish I was. Merle never cared for me as I cared about him."

He cupped her chin in his broad palm and tilted her eyes to meet his. "I'm coming to think we have to be foolish about someone so we can recognize a real love when it crosses our paths." He leaned toward her until the vastness of the sea and the sky vanished. "I'm coming to believe we have to have our hearts broken so real love can slip in and find its place within us. Aveline Lampel, you've been a fool for love, and so have I. I know what I feel for you is the real thing. *Ich liebe dich*, Aveline. I've loved you from the moment you saved me from that guy's knife."

"You've avoided me for the past week."

"I'd like to say it was because I was busy with the harvest, and I was, but your parents don't approve of the man who flirted with every woman he met."

"Every woman but me." She drew away.

"Because you were the only woman who's ever mattered so much to me. I wasn't going to give you an empty-headed answer and an easy smile. I wanted to get to know you because you'd already found your way through the broken shell of my heart."

"Really?"

"*Ja.* If you doubt I'm telling you the truth—" He pulled her to him and kissed her with unhurried pleasure until her toes curled in the heated sand. "Will you marry me, Aveline? We can be foolish together for the rest of our lives."

"*Ja*, I'll marry you, and we can be foolish together," she said before her hand on the back of his head lowered his mouth to hers. In the moment before their lips melded, she whispered, "Starting right after I do the wisest thing I can imagine and kiss you."

Epilogue

~❦~

Snow drifted past the window as Aveline raised the shade to look out. Delight raced through her. Lucas had promised if there was snow on this Sabbath morning, he would hook up the sleigh for their drive to her parents' house where church would start within the hour.

A kiss on her nape beneath her *kapp* sent shivers along her spine. Not cold like the air sneaking past the sash, but warm ones that identified the arms slipping around her as her husband's.

She turned in his arms to link her hands behind his head. "All set to go?"

"It's cold out there. I'm going to need a lot of your kisses to keep me warm on the trip."

"You don't need an excuse to kiss me."

"That's true. I can kiss you whenever I wish." He gave her a quick and loud smack before saying, "We're going to be late, if I get as many kisses as I wish this morning."

"*Ja.*" She left his arms and reached for her heavy black coat. "I'm looking forward to seeing everyone. Nobody is going out with this cold snap. We'll have time to talk with everyone today."

"Not Daryn. Remember? He caught a bus off the Island yesterday."

Aveline remembered how sad Lucas had looked when he'd bid the teen goodbye. With Philip's help, Daryn had found a job on a ranch in Manitoba. He wouldn't be out riding with the cattle herds right away, but he was grateful for being hired to work in the stables.

"I'm going to miss him," she said as she set her black bonnet on her head, "but I'm glad he's following his dream to become a cowboy."

"I don't know if it'll feel that much like a dream come true when the wind is blowing and the snow is falling."

She smiled at him. "It's not your dream or mine, but it's his. Like I said, I'm glad he's going for it. We can talk in the buggy. I don't want to be late, and you know *Mamm* and *Daed* are always happy to see you."

"I thought your *daed* didn't want me around."

"*Daed* has always respected you."

"I realized that after the second incident," he replied, using the term they'd picked up from Philip. "He pulled me aside and let me know how much he appreciated my plan to use the water buffalo to distract the kidnappers. Of course, I never had any idea Moobeam had a scheme of her own."

"You should never underestimate a Lampel female."

"I've learned that, and your *mamm* seems to be coming around. By making my dream of having you for my wife come true, I made your *mamm*'s dream come true."

She laughed as she pulled on her knitted gloves. "Three *kinder* being married the same day. Whoever heard of such a thing?"

"Everyone since that special Tuesday last month." He bent and murmured against her ear, "I thought it would never get to be our turn to exchange our vows."

Nor had she. So many things had surprised her since her move to Prince Edward Island, but nothing more than she would become Lucas's wife. As she put her hand in his and walked out the front door into the blustery day, she knew there was no place where she would rather be than on this Island and with this man.

* * * * *

Dear Reader,

Welcome back to Prince Edward Island for the final time in this miniseries. It's summer, and the flowers are blooming and the potatoes are almost ready to be harvested. I remember those days myself because I spent a good portion of my childhood on a farm in northern New York where we used seed potatoes from…you guessed it! Prince Edward Island.

I've enjoyed writing about this beautiful island, and I hope you've enjoyed the stories as well. In this one, neither Aveline nor Lucas took the easy route to their happy-ever-after, and they had some unexpected adventures along the way. I'll miss writing about the cousins and their families, but now it's time—as the Amish say—to migrate somewhere else.

By the way, the Mennonite Disaster Service which was mentioned in the story is a real organization. It does great and vital work in the aftermath of natural disasters throughout North America.

Visit me at www.joannbrownbooks.com. And look for my next book to see where my characters are turning up next.

Wishing you many blessings,
Jo Ann Brown